TIDES

BOOK TWO
HONOR BOUND

C. Alexander London

SCHOLASTIC INC.

ISBN 978-0-545-66301-4

10 9 8 7 6 5 4 3 2 1   15 16 17 18 19 20/0

Printed in the U.S.A.   40
First printing, January 2015

This one's for my editor, Nick,
a great teammate on land and sea.

PROLOGUE

THE cargo ship sounded the alarm, blasted its water cannons, and sped up as fast as its engines would go.

Its engines would not go fast enough to outrun the pirates.

The pirate warlord known only as Surfer Boy smiled as his three small motorboats accelerated alongside the big ship. His men fired their machine guns into the air, and on deck, the cargo crew ducked and covered, scrambling like roaches caught in the beam of a flashlight.

"Stop your engines!" one of his men shouted

through a bullhorn. "You will now be boarded by the Somali navy."

Surfer Boy laughed at this. They were no more the real navy of Somalia than he was a real blond. He bleached his hair every week to keep it shining bright, almost ghostly white. And Somalia had no true navy.

The pirates answered to no nation or government. They answered only to him.

His man shouted the warning again and Surfer Boy rubbed one hand over his short hair. In his other hand, he held a well-oiled and fully loaded Uzi submachine gun. He nodded at one of his men, who had an AK-47 submachine gun strapped to his back and an MP3 player in his hands. The man hooked the MP3 player up to the speakers on their boat and hit PLAY at full volume.

Playing the Beach Boys as he raided a ship had become a kind of signature for Surfer Boy. Any cargo ship that strayed too close to the shores of Somalia as it passed along the Horn of Africa was in danger of attack by pirates, and no pirate was as feared as Surfer

Boy. He could imagine the terror on the bridge of the cargo ship as they heard the sweet tones of the music gliding across the waves . . . and realized at last who they were up against.

The first boat weaved between the jets of water that the cargo ship used to try to stop the pirates from boarding. The pirates tossed up a grappling hook, and two of them scurried up the lines with guns on their backs, while the other men in the boat continued firing into the air to keep the crew on board ducking low.

Once the first two men were on board, they held the raiding ladder for the rest of the pirates, who scampered up fast, shut off the water cannons, and rushed to find the captain and his officers and hold them at gunpoint until Surfer Boy himself was on board.

By the time Surfer Boy strolled along the deck of the cargo ship, all the crew were his hostages and his men had taken control of the bridge. He stepped inside with a smile on his face, and only when he met the captain eye-to-eye did the blaring Beach Boys song stop.

"Good morning to you, Captain," he said in the sudden silence.

The captain, a gray-haired man with a neatly trimmed beard and a sunburned forehead, stood up tall and tried to stare him down.

But Surfer Boy wouldn't be intimidated. He had been seizing cargo ships and taking hostages for eight years now, and he had met all kinds of captains — brave captains and cowardly captains, captains who cooperated and captains who tried to fight back. Not one of them had impressed him. Before he became a leader of pirates at sea, he had commanded an army on land. He'd fought in Somalia and Yemen and as far away as Afghanistan. He had killed more men than this captain had ever met. The captain's angry stare only made Surfer Boy smile.

"If it's ransom you want," the captain said, "make your demands and get off my ship."

Now Surfer Boy laughed. "Why so hasty? There is no reason we cannot conduct ourselves as gentlemen."

With a smooth motion, he swung his weapon around and pressed the barrel of the submachine gun into the captain's cheek. "Understand?"

The captain nodded. He didn't look so brave now. The metal gun barrel made a little round dent in the captain's soft pink skin.

"Now, tell me, Captain, did you send out a distress signal before we boarded you?" Surfer Boy asked him.

The captain shook his head no.

Surfer Boy pulled the gun away from the man's face. He pointed at the first mate, a younger man, who was being held by two of Surfer Boy's pirates. Without a word, Surfer Boy lowered his gun to the man's foot and pulled the trigger.

Rat tat tat tat tat, the gun barrel spit hot lead.

"Augh!" the first mate screamed as his foot was torn to shreds by the bullets. He fell on his back, rolling in agony, his blood pooling on the metal deck.

The loud shots made Surfer Boy's ears ring like he'd been at a rock concert. It was a feeling he loved.

His two favorite things in the world were the rock 'n' roll music of the Beach Boys and the sound of gunfire. His chosen profession let him enjoy both.

"Why did you do that?" the captain yelled.

"I require your honesty," Surfer Boy said. "Your man will live with a wounded foot. If you lie to me again, I will shoot him in the head."

The captain's face had turned pale.

"Now tell me again," Surfer Boy said. "Did you send a distress signal to the antipiracy task force?"

The captain nodded. "Yes," he said. "I did."

"Exactly how long ago?"

The captain looked at the clock on the wall of the bridge. "Seventeen minutes."

"Good." Surfer Boy checked his watch. "Then the navy will be on their way. We will wait."

The captain looked confused, which was just what Surfer Boy wanted. Confusion in the enemy was a warrior's best friend.

They waited. The pirates kept their guns pointed at the hostages. The first mate clutched his bleeding foot. In less than thirty minutes, Surfer Boy saw a United States Navy warship on the horizon, racing toward them. A helicopter lifted from its deck and sped across the water. One of Surfer Boy's men had slung his gun on his back to free up his hands so he could take notes on everything the navy did.

The radio crackled: "This is Commander Harwell of the USS *Ritland* representing Task Force 151. We have come to negotiate for the release of your hostages. Please respond."

"Wonderful," said Surfer Boy. He checked his watch again. "Thank you for your help, Captain."

He barked an order at his men and one by one, they fell back, withdrawing from the bridge, scampering down the ladders and onto their small boats.

"Please respond," the radio crackled again.

"What about . . . your demands?" the captain asked. "Your ransom?"

"You've given me a greater gift than any ransom." Surfer Boy gave him a playful salute. "I now return your ship."

He followed his men to their boats. Surfer Boy now knew what would happen the next time they took hostages. The ship from counter-piracy Combined Task Force 151 would come, probably this same US Navy vessel, the USS *Ritland*. He knew how long they would take to get there, and that they would deploy a helicopter. They would want to negotiate, to pay him to free the hostages. They would talk and talk and talk.

But Surfer Boy had other plans for the United States Navy the next time they met.

He had his man put on the Beach Boys again as they sped away in their small boats in all different directions.

Let the fools be confused, he thought. *The enemy will never know what hit them.*

As he sped toward the safety of Somali waters, where the US Navy warship dared not follow, Surfer Boy rested his weapon in his lap and laced his fingers behind his bright blond head. He closed his eyes and listened to his favorite song while he dreamed about the bloodshed he was preparing to unleash on the unsuspecting sailors of the United States Navy.

Round round get around . . . I get around.

Wah wah wah wah

Surfer Boy sang right along to the song, laughing all the while.

01:
PARTNERS

THE intruder could come from any direction. He was in full scuba gear, deep below the rolling swells of the Pacific Ocean, and he had only one goal in mind: Don't get caught.

Felix stood in the small inflatable boat on the surface, scanning the ocean through binoculars. The day was bright and clear, with very little chop on the water, and good visibility in all directions. He glanced back at the *Prentiss*, the large US Navy dock landing ship from which he'd been deployed . . . and from which he was being watched by senior officers visiting from all over the country.

Even though he didn't dare look back at them with his binoculars, he knew they were there, taking notes, discussing his performance, and preparing to report back on how he did and — more important — how his partner, Sly, did. It was really up to Sly to catch the intruder after all. Sly was the one hunting in the dark ocean below.

Every few minutes, Felix looked down to the winch and the spool of cable by his feet. The cable unrolled steadily second by second, the towline stretching out into the blue abyss beneath the sun-dappled surface of the water.

"Come on, Sly, you can do it," Felix whispered, willing his partner to succeed. He checked his watch.

Sly had been searching underwater for a while now. He'd popped his head up only once to take a breath, then disappeared again, and Felix had started to wonder what he was doing down there. Hunting for fish? Goofing off?

Having a sea lion for a partner wasn't the easiest thing in the world. Felix couldn't exactly explain to Sly that today's training exercise was especially important. That Special Forces operators and their commanders had come from as far away as Washington, DC, to watch. They were trying to decide the future of the US Navy's Marine Mammal Program. They were trying to decide what to do with sea lions like Sly and sea lion handlers like Felix.

Sly was an experienced search-and-recovery sea lion — one of only thirty-five sea lions in the whole program — but he was still an animal. Some days, Sly liked to let out his wild side, even when the boss was watching and even when a highly trained navy diver, pretending to be an underwater intruder, was doing his best not to let Sly catch him.

"You think he's taking so long because he knows your job is on the line?" Gutierrez asked. "Or does he just like the drama?"

Felix shrugged.

Gutierrez was the boat driver, a boatswain's mate, but he knew that it'd be easy for him to get a new assignment if they shut down the Marine Mammal

Program. They were in the navy. Everyone needed a boat driver.

As for Petty Officer Second Class Felix Pratt, he didn't know what he'd do outside the program. All his skills were related to training and taking care of Sly. If they shut down the sea lion teams, what need would there be for a Marine Mammal Systems Operator? Put another way, why would the navy need a guy who knew how to brush a sea lion's teeth?

Of course, Felix could do other things. He was a great swimmer. He'd competed on the US national swim team when he was in high school. He didn't make it to the Olympics, but he was faster than most guys he knew. Not as fast as a sea lion — they could swim up to twenty-five miles per hour — but still, for a person, Felix was like lightning. He'd been a life-guard almost every summer since he was fifteen, so he knew CPR and first aid, and he was a certified scuba diver himself.

Surely, he thought, the navy would find a good job for someone like him if they closed the Marine

Mammal Program. But he did wonder what would happen to Sly. Would he be sent to a zoo or an aquarium? Released into the wild?

When a person imagined a seal in the circus balancing a ball on its nose, they were probably imagining a California sea lion just like Sly. If the military program was shut down, Felix feared Sly would be sold to a circus, although that wasn't really likely. But he couldn't be released into the wild, either.

Sly had lived his whole life in captivity with humans looking after all his needs. In their natural habitat, seals and sea lions like Sly fought one another for dominance in their groups, fought other groups for access to the best hunting territory, and did their best to keep from falling prey to the larger animals that hunted them, like killer whales and sharks. Felix couldn't imagine that kind of life for Sly. He was as much a navy sailor as he was a wild animal.

"Come on, pal," Felix whispered, checking his watch again. Navy sailors who can't do their jobs don't keep those jobs for long. Even big, furry, fish-smelling sailors like Sly.

Just then, there came a jolt on the spooling line. Seconds later, there was a flash of brown fur on the surface, and Sly burst up from the water, his dark eyes shining.

All six hundred pounds of him leaped from the ocean and slid onto the long mat on the front of the boat. He walked forward on his flippers, sat back on his rear, and opened his mouth wide, barking his high-pitched sea lion bark. He wore a bright orange nylon harness. It was his uniform, and when the uniform went on, Sly knew it was time to work. Now that his work was done, he knew it was time for his reward.

"Woo-hoo!" Felix cheered, and tossed his partner a chunk of fish from a cooler. Sly caught it in the air and swallowed it with one gulp.

"Let's reel in our catch," Felix said, and the driver pressed a button, which started spooling the long cable back in toward the boat. Felix got on his radio and reported that Sly had caught the target.

Another gray inflatable boat came speeding in their direction. On board, a team of navy maritime police was armed and ready to arrest the intruder, or pretend to. It was all part of the training exercise.

After a few minutes, the large clamp at the end of the cable came into view — along with the diver, who had been dragged to the surface with the clamp locked around his leg. It had been placed there by Sly, in the dark at sixty feet below the surface.

The police hauled the diver onto their boat, unlocked the clamp, and simulated placing him under arrest.

"Wooeee!" the diver shouted across the water to the boat where Felix and Sly were standing side by side, beaming proudly at their work. "I thought I was going to make it," the diver said. "I didn't even see him coming for me down there. It was so dark. All of a sudden, I felt something snap on my leg and I looked back and the big guy was right there. I thought he'd bit me!"

"Nah," Felix called back. "Sly doesn't bite. He used his mouth to put that clamp on you."

The diver laughed while pulling off his fins and his mask. "By the time I felt the cable start to pull me to the surface, he was already gone. I saw maybe just the tip of his tail as he swam back. I'll tell you, he's one heck of a seal."

"So are you," Felix laughed. "Don't be too hard on yourself!"

The diver was a Navy SEAL instructor, one of the best combat scuba divers in the navy and one of the most elite special warfare operators in the whole US military. In the course of his career, he had swum silently onto enemy beaches and boarded hostile ships undetected, all over the world.

But he couldn't sneak past Sly.

As they motored back to the *Prentiss*, Felix patted Sly's thick fur with a satisfying slapping sound. The sea lion rolled over on his mat, like a dog would, and let Felix scratch the spot where his flippers met his body. It was Sly's favorite spot.

"Sly's the best," Felix said, and put his hand up for a high five, which Sly returned.

"You got that right!" Gutierrez shouted over the engine sound, glancing up toward the *Prentiss*, where all the visiting officers were watching them from the deck. "He probably just saved our jobs."

"Of course he did," Felix called back. "We're partners! He's got my back, just like I've got his. Always."

The sea lion barked, almost like he understood.

02:
MISSION READY

FELIX and Sly were just two members of the MK 6 Marine Mammal team, or "Mark 6," a unit of the navy's Explosive Ordnance Disposal Group. They were based out of San Diego, where they were responsible for patrolling the port to prevent civilian trespassers — or even terrorist attacks by sea. They were also occasionally tasked with recovering equipment from the dark ocean floor and searching for mines and other underwater explosives, jobs that would be next to impossible without Sly's amazing underwater vision. In addition to handlers like Felix and boat operators like Gutierrez, there were other members of the team — veterinarians and their staff, interns from the local university, civilian animal trainers, equipment specialists, and officers to command the whole group. It took a lot of people — and a lot of money — to maintain the program.

The most important relationship, though, was between the handler and his partner. They spent the most time together, working on skills and signals, learning to trust each other, practicing their duties under all different conditions, and even playing together to keep their friendship strong. While a lot of other people were responsible for Sly's health and well-being, Felix felt as though Sly was his personal responsibility. He often annoyed the veterinarians because he asked so many questions. He wanted to know as much as he could, so he would be ready to help Sly in an emergency if he ever had to.

"It's not like you'll be in combat," Gutierrez had told him once. "We're defensive. We guard ships; we don't attack terrorists."

"I just like to be prepared," said Felix.

"You just like extra work," said Gutierrez.

The Marine Mammal team had set up big inflatable water tanks in the hull of the *Prentiss*, and Sly was back in his within minutes of coming on board. The veterinarians had checked him out and given him a clean bill of health while the Navy SEAL diver changed into dry clothes to go brief the commanders about his experience getting caught by a sea lion. Felix would be called to brief the officers soon, too, but now that Sly was settled in, he had to write up a report about the training exercise. There was a lot of paperwork for a Marine Mammal Systems Operator. It wasn't a glamorous job.

The *Prentiss* motored back to Naval Base Point Loma. Once they got there, the MK 6 team returned Sly to his pen in the bay, where the conditions were much better than in the mobile tank on board the ship. The tank was like a big inflatable kiddie pool, but Sly's pen on the base was a big square of underwater netting, which kept Sly safe while allowing the real ocean to flow in and out. It was much more like the environment in which Sly would live in the wild, and there were other sea lions there, as well as dolphins in similar pens nearby, and they all made noises at one another, communicating in those mysterious ways that mammals of the sea have.

Felix wondered if humans would ever understand what these intelligent creatures were saying to one another. He also wondered if humans would ever really want to. After all, how would they keep animals like this in pens and tanks and make them work for fish if they could understand what the animals were saying? What if they said they didn't like being in the navy at all?

Felix looked at Sly rolling around and around in his pen, seemingly happily. He smiled at his partner. The sea lion looked to be enjoying himself just fine. He had all these people looking after him, and the fish the navy fed him were even better quality than what most restaurants served. It wasn't such a bad life for a sea lion at all.

While Sly enjoyed a well-deserved break, Felix finished his paperwork and reported to his commander as ordered.

"Nice job today," she told him. "You did well."

"Thank you, Commander," Felix said. "Sly deserves all the credit. I just pass out the fish."

"You're being modest," she told him. It wasn't a compliment so much as a statement of fact. Commander Jackson was a career naval officer who had graduated at the top of her class from the Naval Academy in Annapolis and had risen quickly through the ranks. She'd deployed to help victims of the tsunami in Asia and she'd deployed on an aircraft carrier to support the war in Iraq. Now that she was in the peaceful waters of San Diego Bay, she expected as much hard work and focus from her team as she had in combat.

"You impressed some of the Spec Ops," she said, referring to the senior officers from the Special Operations Division who had watched the demonstration.

"I've got a request for one Mark Six team to deploy to Task Force 151 out of Bahrain."

Felix knew that Bahrain was a port in the Middle East where the US Navy had a base, but he had no idea what Task Force 151 was or why they should need a sea lion team.

Commander Jackson must have seen the puzzled look cross Felix's face. "They're an antipiracy task force," she explained. "They patrol the waters off the coast of Somalia. Their official mission is to deter and disrupt the armed pirates operating in those waters."

She pushed a file folder over to Felix. CLASSIFIED was stamped across the cover of the file. Felix had security clearance to see classified documents at this level of secrecy, but there was still a policy of "need to know." He was only supposed to see classified files if he needed to know what was in them in order to perform his job.

"Take a look and see what you think," Commander Jackson said. "I've put in your name for this mission. You and the support team will deploy in two weeks.

Official orders to come, but I wanted to give you a heads-up. This is not a traditional mission for a Marine Mammal team." Commander Jackson laced her fingers together and leaned forward, locking eyes with him. "And this might be our last chance to show what the Marine Mammal Program can do."

"Last chance, ma'am?" Felix asked.

She nodded. "I've received word that they are still considering shutting us down and replacing the animals with robotic underwater drones. They're cheaper to maintain and, well, the animal rights people can't object to the navy using robots."

"But . . ." Felix was at a loss for words. He'd just demonstrated the amazing work Sly could do. Surely no underwater robot could have done so well? And he knew that animal rights groups had objected to the navy's Marine Mammal Program, but the animals were well cared for — loved, even — so the idea that the navy was somehow abusing them by giving them a job to do was unfair. The animals were treated better than the human sailors!

"I understand your surprise," Commander Jackson told him. "And I would ask you to please keep this information to yourself. Nothing is decided yet, and I believe, if you and Sly do a good job with the anti-piracy task force, that we can show just how valuable and necessary the program remains."

"No pressure, ma'am," Felix said, a little bit of sarcasm in his voice. Her face hardened, and he really wished he hadn't just run off his mouth. He'd been like that ever since elementary school: always making that one extra comment he didn't need to make. It always got him into trouble.

"You are the best sea lion handler in the United States Navy," Commander Jackson said. "I should think you can handle a little pressure. If not, I can always find someone else for this assignment."

"No, ma'am." Felix straightened his back. "I'm ready to represent our program to the best of Sly's abilities. Thank you, ma'am."

Even though he'd been scolded, he swelled a bit with pride as he picked up the file and the commander dismissed him. She had just called him the best. She was deploying him to the other side of the world to try to save the Marine Mammal Program from being shut down.

As he walked back down the docks to check in on Sly, he held the file tightly in his hand, eager to flip through it and see what it said.

Pirates, he thought. *Real-life pirates.*

He knew that they weren't pirates like in the movies, with eye patches and parrots. They were ragtag bands of criminals in rickety boats who seized cargo ships, held hostages, and demanded ransom from the big companies that owned the ships. They stole millions of dollars a year this way. They had more in common with kidnappers and gangsters than they did with fictional pirates like Captain Hook or Jack Sparrow.

Felix got down to the pier where the marine mammals lived, flashed his ID even though everyone knew him, and strolled along, breathing deep the salty air, listening to the gentle slap of water against the dock.

He reached Sly's area and sat down on the trainer's platform. Sly, who had sprawled out in a patch of sun, lifted his big brown head up from the float he was lying on and sniffed at the air, his long whiskers twitching. Felix didn't make a move toward the orange harness hanging on a peg or the locker that held the training toys, so Sly knew it wasn't time to work. He flopped his head right back down to rest again. There was nothing sea lions loved more than sunbathing.

Felix looked past the sea lion to the light dappling the surface of the bay of San Diego. He watched the big ships at their moorings, the small boats racing about between them like bees flitting between flowers. On the distant beach, he saw a group of men in training, soaking wet and covered in sand, carrying a big rubber boat over their heads. In the air, a squadron of cargo helicopters thrummed in formation toward the horizon. It was the bustle of activity that kept a military organization as large and complicated as the United States Navy working. This was just one base among thousands all over the world, and Felix was just one sailor among hundreds of thousands, doing one job among the thousands that people in the navy performed every day.

Except Felix had been asked by his commanding officer to play a new role, and his heart beat a little faster in his chest as he prepared to find out what that role might be. He leaned back and opened the classified file. The commander's words echoed in his head: *This is not a traditional mission for a Marine Mammal team.*

As he read, he knew right away what she meant. The navy had guidelines and rules and policies in place to keep the mammals in their program out of harmful or hostile situations as much as possible. This new mission would put both him and Sly right into the middle of very hostile situations . . . exactly what the animal rights people were worried about. The assignment would put them on the front lines in the war against pirates in the Arabian Sea, but it would also give Sly an important role in saving the lives of the pirates' hostages. It was a chance for them to do some real good, all the way on the other side of the world.

Felix knew that Sly could do the job that the task force needed him to do, and that he could do it well, and that in doing it well, he could save the whole program.

But he also knew it would be dangerous.

"We eat danger for breakfast, don't we, Sly?" Felix said out loud.

The sea lion lifted his pointy nose and looked across the water to Felix again, but quickly put it back down when no signal to do anything came. The sea lion probably knew by now that his handler sometimes just talked for the sake of talking. He went back to enjoying his well-earned nap in the sun.

"Rest up, pal," Felix said. "You're going to need it."

03:
OPERATION SUSHI ROLL

THE MK 6 sea lion team could have deployed within seventy-two hours of receiving their orders, but they didn't. Commander Jackson didn't want to alarm anyone in the community of veterinarians, researchers, students, and animal care advisors who supported the Marine Mammal Program. She didn't want to draw any attention to the mission Felix and Sly were about to begin.

"We will take every step necessary for the protection of the animals in our care, but the fewer personnel involved in this mission, the better," Commander Jackson told Felix in what had become a regular predeployment briefing. They had so many meetings that Felix began to wonder if he was a sea lion handler or a meeting handler. The commander was clearly anxious for Felix to do well.

A lieutenant commander from DEVGRU — also known as SEAL Team Six, the most elite unit of Navy Special Forces soldiers — came to brief Felix and to watch him train with Sly over the course of the two weeks before they took off for the Arabian Sea.

His name was Lt. Commander Barcott and he asked a lot of questions, took a lot of notes, and whispered to members of his staff, but he never explained to Felix exactly why he was there. Commander Jackson seemed to know, though, and Felix trusted her. If she didn't think he needed to know what Lt. Commander Barcott was up to, then he didn't need to know.

Everyone else on the MK 6 team knew only that they were meant to prepare for the deployment to the port in Bahrain, in the Middle East. Most of them did not know why.

They did know that they had to get the mobile tanks assembled, tested, and disassembled again. They had to prepare the onboard sea lion cages, the rigid-hull inflatable boats, or "RHIBs," the medical supplies and coolers of fish, training tools and toys, and, of course, their own gear, and they had to load it all onto a big C-130 cargo plane. The plane would take a crew of about twenty of them to the Middle East.

There, the members of MK 6 would be assigned to the USS *Ritland*, a Wasp-class amphibious assault ship, usually one of the first on the scene when pirates seized a private cargo vessel or tourist sailboat at sea. The *Ritland* could hold an entire United States Marine Corps expeditionary force if it had to. It was the sort of ship from which you could invade a country.

"What use could they have for Sly?" Gutierrez asked Felix on the afternoon before they were scheduled to fly out. "We're not a combat unit. We're Support Systems. What mission are we supposed to support in pirate waters?"

Felix and Gutierrez were floating together on a thirty-foot rubber boat with a big engine. They had Sly's equipment on board and his cage — a crate almost like the kind you'd put a dog in. Sly would rest comfortably inside until it was time to work.

"You joined the navy during wartime, G." Felix smiled. "What'd you expect, boat rides and sight-seeing?"

"That is exactly what I expected," said Gutierrez. "And a college loan."

"But you're part of the US Navy!" Felix threw his arms in the air in an exaggerated show of excitement. "A global force for good."

That was the navy's recruitment motto on all the TV ads. The thing was, even though he said it as a joke, Felix believed it.

He wanted to be a part of a global force for good. He wanted to be a hero. He had been getting bored with all the training exercises in the San Diego Bay, all the search and recovery missions looking for old World War II—era sea mines. He knew that he — and Sly —

could do more than just find lost equipment. He was eager to get the chance.

"Let's do this drill one more time," said Felix.

Gutierrez grumbled as he picked up the radio to call the other boat. "I wish they'd tell us what this drill was for."

And Felix wished he could tell him, wished he could reveal just how important their mission was. But he'd been told to keep it to himself.

There were five guys on the other boat, a rickety wooden thing with two outsized engines. It was a simulated pirate boarding vessel, just like the boats the Somali pirates used to attack cargo ships, and at Gutierrez's radio signal, they were going to stage a pretend attack on an imaginary ship.

"We're go for attack," he said into the radio. Then he turned to Felix. "And we're go for Operation . . . uh . . . What's this called?"

"Sushi Roll."

"Operation Sushi Roll?" Gutierrez shook his head. "Who'd name a mission after raw fish and rice?"

Felix shrugged. "It wasn't my idea."

Gutierrez revved the engine and they sped off. Felix could feel his heartbeat racing. He knew the exercise was only a drill, but this was their last time to run through it before they might have to do the same thing during a real pirate attack. He wanted to make sure he got everything right.

When the rickety boarding vessel was in sight, Gutierrez slowed and turned their boat away to keep a safe distance.

Felix opened Sly's cage and the sea lion came hopping out on his four flippers. His whole body bounced as he walked the few steps to Felix. Felix held his hand up in the stop signal and Sly stopped, sitting back on his haunches like a dog. Felix tossed him a small fish, which he swallowed in one quick bite.

The sea lion had been trained to do his job in small steps. First he learned to get into and out of his cage, then to stop when Felix told him to stop. Next he learned to take the equipment in his mouth and, eventually, he learned to deposit it where he was instructed, to tug on it to make sure it was attached firmly, and to swim back to Felix and signal that he'd done his job. Each step had taken weeks, sometimes months of training, during which Felix patiently ignored Sly's mistakes and rewarded him when he got it right. It took years of training just to prepare one sea lion to be a member of the MK 6 team.

In the last two weeks, Sly had been required to apply what he'd learned over all those years to a totally new situation. Felix was impressed by how quickly the animal had adapted and by how hard he worked to get it right. Felix wondered if Sly just loved the fish rewards that much, or if there was something else, something deeper motivating the animal — something like pride. Could sea lions take pride in a job well done? Did Sly even know he had a job, or was this all play to him?

Felix gave Sly a small magnetic tracking beacon attached to a clamp. Once Sly had it in his mouth, Felix made a big gesture and the sea lion hopped his way to the edge of the boat and leaped into the water. In a flash, he was gone, racing beneath the surface on an intercept course with the pirate boat.

In just a few minutes, he was back, barking happily on board and asking for his reward.

"Did we get it?" Felix asked.

Gutierrez checked the laptop next to the steering wheel.

"Roger that," he said. "The beacon is attached and we are tracking the pirates."

A voice crackled over the radio. "You kidding me?" it said. "He did it already? We didn't see a thing."

"Mission accomplished," Felix said, giving Sly an affectionate pat on his side. The sea lion barked again, a happy, high-pitched noise.

Felix hoped his partner stayed just as quick and just as happy when they had to do this for real, with real pirates, who had real guns . . . and who wouldn't hesitate to shoot a sea lion if they caught him.

04:
PICKUP GAME

THE sun was like a ball of fire overhead, the ocean like a mirror below, and the USS *Ritland* floated in between, sizzling on the sea. Day after day, Felix and the rest of the Marine Mammal team sweated and sweltered along with their new shipmates, and day after day, not much else happened. It was just hot.

The navy task force patrolled a large stretch of ocean off the coast of Africa, and the *Ritland* seemed to be always on the move but never headed anywhere specific. Sometimes they would hear the high-pitched buzz of an unmanned drone aircraft flying overhead, and Felix knew it was sending pictures of the whole area to a control room, where intelligence officers could see all the cargo ships and fishing boats in the area, as well as anything that looked like a threat. But they must never have seen anything threatening, because the drones kept on flying past and the ship didn't speed up or change course to follow them.

Once a day, the *Ritland* would stop so that Felix and Sly could practice, giving Sly a chance to get out of his pool and flex his flippers in the open ocean. Crew members would stand along the rails on deck to watch. They'd call out for him to do tricks. Felix would run through the training with toys and with fish and the guys would applaud, but Felix never actually made Sly do any tricks. Sly wasn't a performer in some SeaWorld show. He was a valuable and talented member of the navy, and Felix felt like the sailors owed the animal some respect. He didn't say that, though. He let them think Sly was entertaining them when he was really just doing his job.

Guys wanted to come up to pet Sly, and Felix would warn them off.

"He doesn't like strangers," Felix would explain.

"What are you talking about?" Gutierrez whispered to Felix the first time it happened. "Sly loves strangers."

"I know," Felix whispered back as he gestured for Sly to hop back into his crate so they could wheel him belowdecks again. "I just don't want them treating Sly like a pet or a ship's mascot or something. He's a professional."

"He's a sea lion," Gutierrez said.

"He can be both," Felix responded. "Did you know they give military working dogs ranks? Whatever rank the dog handler is, the dog gets one rank higher, so they're always treated with respect. There are German shepherds in the army with the rank of sergeant. I think there's even a Labrador who's a marine corps major."

"No way."

"It's true," said Felix. "I wish they'd do the same for our program."

"Nah," Gutierrez disagreed. "I got enough commanding officers to take orders from. I don't need to be outranked by a sea lion."

"Why not?" Felix smiled. "You already drive him around."

"Well, I'm not calling Sly *sir*," Gutierrez told him.

"You don't even call your commanding officers *sir*," Felix teased. "Why would you start with Sly?"

"Guess you're right," Gutierrez laughed. "Though Sly's got better breath than Commander Jackson."

Felix rolled his eyes, but didn't dignify Gutierrez's comment with a response.

"And he sure is friendlier than Lieutenant Greff," Gutierrez added, with a glance back to make sure no one was listening in on their conversation. He whispered, "I think Sly's smarter, too."

Lieutenant Greff was their commanding officer while they were on board the USS *Ritland*. He made sure the Mark 6 team had everything they needed to stay fit and alert, and he relayed to them any orders that came down from the ship's captain.

The orders were never all that interesting. Most days they were just schedules of when Sly's team would get to take the small boat out for training, when they needed to be back on board the ship, and when in the schedule they got their breaks, their meals, and their free time. Lieutenant Greff didn't seem to have much interest in the particulars of their training routine, and he had never interacted directly with Sly — not even on their first meeting, when Felix had signaled the sea lion to use his flipper to salute the lieutenant.

The lieutenant had not appeared to find that amusing.

"He is mission ready?" Lieutenant Greff had said, without even acknowledging the furry brown animal staring up at him.

"Yes, sir," Felix had answered, gesturing for Sly to lower his flipper. He had given the sea lion a fish and tried to act as if nothing had happened. He knew now that Lieutenant Greff was a hard-nosed man with no real affection for the animal team he was now responsible for. Luckily, the lieutenant kept his distance once they were on board. In fact, he was almost too distant. The man never once came down to the cargo hold where the team had set up. And Felix was instructed to send his daily updates by email. After his regular face-to-face meetings with Commander Jackson back in California, it was an unsatisfying way to communicate with his supervisor.

Felix assumed Lieutenant Greff read all his emails, plus the training reports and the veterinarian reports, but he didn't know for sure. He hoped the lieutenant was at least sending the reports on so that the officers above him would know that Felix and Sly were doing well. It wasn't their fault no pirates had come along yet.

The days went on like that for a while. Training and idle talk with his boat driver. Checkups with the veterinarian, writing emails to Lieutenant Greff, then more training.

Otherwise, nothing much happened. They received no distress calls from ships under siege by pirates. They received no new orders. All Felix and the rest of the sea lion team could do was wait.

Lt. Commander Barcott and his SEAL team weren't even on board.

"Don't worry about them," Commander Jackson told Felix when he called her over webcam for an update. It was funny to see his commander's face right there on his laptop when she was on the other side of the world. "They can be there in a matter of hours if they are needed. Let's hope they are not needed."

Felix's face must have shown some disappointment.

"It is a *good* thing if there are no pirate attacks," Commander Jackson scolded him.

"But, ma'am," Felix said, "if there are no pirate attacks, then we've got no chance to demonstrate what Sly can do. It won't help the program."

"Sailor." Commander Jackson shook her head. "If there are no pirate attacks, then no one is in danger. I know you want to do a good job out there, but don't lose sight of your priorities."

"Aye aye, ma'am," Felix agreed unconvincingly, then finished updating her about Sly, how he was adjusting to life aboard the ship, what he was eating, how his practice was going . . . all the normal stuff. When the call was done, Felix went below to check in with his partner.

Sly looked about as bored as Felix was.

The sea lion had his own cargo hold in the belly of the *Ritland*. There was a mobile clinic where the veterinarian could attend to his every need; there were freezers full of high-quality fish; there were lockers filled with toys and supplies; and then there was the big pool, where Sly swam and lounged and played. It was surrounded by netting so he couldn't jump out and wouldn't fall out when the ocean got rough. High up above the pool, attached to the netting, there was a basketball hoop.

"If we can't do anything else," Felix said aloud, "we might as well have some fun."

Felix pulled a big red ball from one of the lockers and made his way toward Sly's pool, holding the ball over his head. Sly had been napping on a platform just above the water, which was like a diving board that didn't bounce. As soon as Felix drew near, though, the sea lion jumped onto his flippers, wide-awake, and dove into the water. In a flash, he was at the water's edge, his brown snout poking over the lip of the pool, his white whiskers bristling in the air, and his wide black eyes, ringed with long eyelashes, fixed on the ball. Sly was ready to play.

Felix unzipped the netting and climbed onto the edge of the pool, where he could sit with his feet dangling in the water. He hung a small cooler of fish off the outside of the pool. Then he held the ball over his head and Sly stood his body straight up out of the water, front flippers raised like he was saying *I'm open! Pass me the ball!*

Felix looked around. The veterinarian wasn't there. Her assistant was busying himself with paperwork and paid no attention. He'd seen this game a thousand times. But some of the sailors in the cargo hold had turned to watch. For them, this was totally new. They'd been working belowdecks and never got to see Sly in training in the ocean.

If they want tricks, thought Felix, *I'll give them tricks. Looks like it's the closest to a demonstration of his skills as we're gonna get.*

Felix tossed the ball into the air, and Sly batted it down with his flipper. In one smooth motion, he dove below it, shot out of the water while balancing the ball at the end of his nose, and headbutted it up into the basket.

Nothing but net.

The sailors applauded. Sly gripped the ball in his mouth and swam it back to Felix. With a flick of his head, he tossed the ball up and Felix caught it. The sea lion raised his flippers and applauded Felix's catch. That sent the sailors into hysterics.

Felix reached back into the cooler and tossed Sly a fish. Then he raised the ball up and, with his other arm, made a gesture like he was pulling a rope. Sly did a quick flip underwater and raced across the tank. Felix tossed the ball and Sly leaped, catching it in mid-air before diving back in with a splash.

"Can he dunk?" one of the sailors shouted.

"He can dunk you!" another replied.

Felix didn't answer them. He kept his attention on his partner and leaned out to pat the surface of the water, calling Sly back to him for the next game. Sly circled the tank with the ball in his mouth, happy as a sea lion could be.

Suddenly, a red light over the door to the cargo hold lit up and a siren sounded, loud and long: *OOO EEE OOO EEE OOO EEE.*

Felix, still leaning over the water, startled, slipped, and fell, splashing into Sly's pool.

Sly rushed to him, knocking Felix with his snout and his flippers, nudging him back up to the surface.

When Felix burst up again, only a moment had passed, but the other sailors were rushing about, securing equipment, running to their posts, calling out quick instructions to one another.

"Get out of the tank and dry off, double-time!" the veterinarian's assistant shouted up at Felix. He was standing by the wall, holding a phone receiver in his hand. "We're on."

It took Felix a moment to realize what the guy meant by "we're on."

The officer on the other end of the phone was telling the sea lion team to engage Counter-Piracy Condition Bravo. Or, said another way: battle stations.

Pirates were attacking a cargo ship, and the USS *Ritland* had been called to the rescue.

05:
INTERCEPT COURSE

THE *Ritland* cut the waves at thirty knots, racing to intercept the cargo ship that had sent out the distress signal. Crew scrambled to prepare, manning their battle stations. Down below, corpsmen prepared the medical clinic for any casualties.

The cargo ship in trouble was an American freighter out of Norfolk, Virginia, called the *Duchess*. It was hauling electronics, building supplies, and five thousand tons of emergency food donations for hungry people in East Africa. It had an American crew.

All of that meant that the news media back in the United States would be very interested in the story if they found out that the ship had been hijacked by pirates. And if the news media got interested in the story, that would mean that members of Congress and the president would be interested in it, too, which meant that if this pirate attack wasn't stopped quickly, the top leadership of the military would be breathing down the neck of the captain of the USS *Ritland* to take care of the situation. The captain would be breathing down the senior officers' necks, and they, in turn, would be breathing down everyone else's necks and everyone on board would be tense.

It was a lot of pressure, but it was also the perfect opportunity to show everyone how good he could be, how good Sly could be, and how irreplaceable the navy's sea lion teams really were. This was his chance to shine.

The first thing he had to do, though, was change into a dry uniform.

He put on new camo utilities and rushed back to the cargo hold to help the rest of his team get Sly prepped for their mission.

To his surprise, Lieutenant Greff was standing in the cargo hold. It was the first time Felix had ever seen him belowdecks.

"Sir." Felix gave him a crisp salute.

"The SEALs are en route," the lieutenant told Felix. "They'll be making an aerial entry at twenty hundred, and once on board, Commander Barcott will brief you on the particulars of this operation. The SEAL team will assume operational command of this mission and you will take your instructions from his people, understood?"

"Yes, sir," Felix replied. He checked his watch. Twenty hundred was military time for 8:00 p.m. Two hours away. Aerial entry meant that the Navy SEALs would be skydiving into the water under cover of night and boarding the *Ritland* while they were still moving to intercept the pirate attack. That way, the ship wouldn't have to stop to pick them up. Operational command meant that the SEALs would be in charge, which meant this was a mission where they expected danger. Why else put navy frogmen in charge of it?

Those guys didn't even bother to get out of bed for anything less than deadly.

Felix's mouth felt dry. It looked like he was finally getting to do something more than train and fill out paperwork, but it was all happening so fast. His heart thumped in his rib cage. He was nervous. He was excited. He needed to calm down, to focus, to relax. Sea lions could sense tension, and they didn't like it. The most important thing for the health and safety of an animal like Sly was to keep him relaxed, and for that to happen, Felix had to stay relaxed himself.

"Get your team ready to deploy," Lieutenant Greff said. "Then meet me in the command center."

"Aye aye, sir," said Felix, and with that, Lieutenant Greff turned on his heels and left the sea lion team to do its work.

They let Sly stay in his pool for as long as they could, but eventually it was time to bring the sea lion out. Felix checked his watch. An hour had passed. There was another hour left until the SEALs arrived.

The team unzipped the netting and Felix signaled Sly to climb out of the tank. The sea lion quickly obeyed and Felix rewarded him with a fish. The noise of the roaring engines, the blaring sirens, and the combat-ready crew running about seemed to startle the sea lion now that he was out of his pool. The tiny nubs he had for ears twitched on the side of his head and his eyes darted around the wide open space.

Felix stood in front of him and reassured him, then pointed to the crate a few feet away. When Sly saw his crate, he immediately scuttled over to it, shaking the water from his brown fur before he went inside and seemed instantly to relax again. Felix knew that most animals like routine. They like familiar activities and people and places they recognize. They do not like surprises. It was Felix's job, in the midst of a pirate attack, to keep Sly from being surprised.

They followed normal procedure, as if it were just another training exercise, wheeling Sly's crate on deck, then onto the small boat. Gutierrez was there already, getting the vessel ready to launch into the water.

"This for real?" Gutierrez asked.

"It's for real," Felix said.

The boat launch guys were checking ropes and securing the ramp, moving like a well-oiled machine.

Felix checked his watch. He looked up at the sky, but he knew he wouldn't hear or see anything. The SEALs would drop from the clouds in silence and would be on board the *Ritland* before anyone knew anything about it.

Felix used the time he had left before meeting Lieutenant Greff and Lt. Commander Barcott at the command center to go over checklists with Gutierrez, to comfort Sly inside his crate, and to check in with Dr. Morris, the veterinarian, to make sure she was ready to spring into action should Sly be hurt.

"You should know," she told Felix, "I do not approve of this mission, nor of using Sly in this way."

"Yes, ma'am," Felix said. The veterinarian was an officer and it was not Felix's place to contradict her. In truth, he wasn't sure why she was confiding in him now.

"But there is nothing you or I can do about it except look after that animal as best we can," she continued.

"Yes, ma'am," Felix repeated.

"You're young," she said. "And I know this is your first operation like this. I can tell you're excited. Do not let that excitement cloud your judgment." She locked eyes with Felix. "You are responsible for your partner's well-being and his safe return. Let the special operations folks worry about the rest of the mission. You do your job and keep Sly safe. Understood?"

Felix nodded, then caught himself, and repeated once again, "Yes, ma'am."

He was tired of all these officers lecturing him. He just wanted to get out on the water and do what he and Sly had been training to do. He wanted to make a difference. He wanted to show they really were the best and that no robotic drone could replace them. He'd do whatever it took to prove that.

"Dismissed," the veterinarian said. "And good luck, sailor."

"Thank you, ma'am," Felix said, and made his way from the cargo hold toward the command center. He didn't dare let the veterinarian see his face as he walked away, because he was smiling.

He was ready. Sly was ready.

And Felix couldn't wait to receive his orders from the commander of the Navy SEALs to take his sea lion out on the open water and do his part in the fight against pirates.

A global force for good, Felix thought. *Bring it on.*

06:
PIRATES AND PLANS

M ODERN-DAY pirates share a few things in common with other pirates throughout history.

In the golden age of piracy, when Spanish galleons heavy with treasure from the New World sailed the Caribbean, those who lived outside the law saw a great opportunity on the high seas. But ships were expensive, and not just anyone could get one.

Often, wealthy and powerful people would provide the money for pirate ships, and they would recruit eager sailors, bored aristocrats, daring adventurers, discontented outcasts, and wanted criminals to serve as the crew.

These pirate ships were purely money-making investments, with the crew pledging to serve together, loot, pillage, and steal, then split the profits according to an agreed-upon deal with the wealthy investors. At the start of every voyage, the Articles of Piracy would be signed or marked by everyone on their crew. These articles provided a code of conduct for the pirates; they spelled out the rations of food and water and rum that each would get, how their votes would be counted, and how their share of the gold would be split. If the ship captured good ransom on their voyage, everyone made money. If they didn't, no one did. Unlike in the navy, pirate captains could be voted out by their crew if they failed to lead the ship to riches. It was good motivation for every pirate, from the captain to the deckhands, to work hard at their violent profession on the high seas.

These pirate ships were sometimes even commissioned by governments to attack ships sailing under the flag of other governments. Piracy became a way for countries to wage war against one another at sea without having to raise a naval fleet, pay their sailors, or take responsibility for their actions.

In the old days, nearly anyone could sign on to a pirate ship, as long as they could contribute something useful. There were young pirates and old pirates, black pirates and white pirates, male pirates and female pirates (though the latter were not common). There were Jewish, Christian, and Muslim pirates all working side by side.

At a time when the world was hardly equal among men and women and people of different races and religions, pirate ships were some of the most equitable places on earth. Everyone was paid according to the work they did, from the captain to the cabin boys. Of course, the owners of the ships didn't have to risk their lives sailing on board with the pirates if they didn't want to. They only needed to risk their money, and they got paid handsomely from the pirates' loot before any of the pirates got their cut. They also stood less risk of being caught and hanged for piracy, which, in spite of its articles and codes of conduct, was still illegal and punishable by death. Some ports, like New Providence in the Bahamas and Tortuga in the Caribbean, became pirate havens, where men like Jean Lafitte, Blackbeard, and Calico Jack could live openly as criminal heroes.

Today, the goals of piracy are not all that different from what they were in the age of sailing ships. Pirates still hijack ships at sea in order to make money, but now, instead of stealing gold and treasure, they take hostages and demand ransom to release them. Unlike the pirates of old, modern pirates have cell phones and secret bank accounts, and they don't carry cutlasses. They carry machine guns.

There still are pirate havens, but these havens are no longer in the Caribbean. Nowadays, most modern pirates make their home along the coast of the African country of Somalia, where they can raid the rich shipping lanes of the Arabian Sea.

Pirates don't vote for their leaders anymore, either. Their leaders are usually criminals and warlords, who also take most of the ransom money wired directly into their bank accounts. The pirates themselves usually come from small fishing villages by the water, where it's hard to make a good living catching fish.

The warlords recruit poor young men — it's always young men now — who don't have many other options for employment. These small crews take cheap boats with big motors out to attack passing ships — Chinese fishing boats, Saudi oil tankers, American cargo ships. They board the ships, take the crew hostage at gunpoint, and demand payment or else they'll start shooting people.

Unlike pirates of olden times, modern pirates rarely actually kill anyone. They see their piracy as a business. The ships' owners use their insurance money to pay off the ransom; the warlords score millions of dollars; their pirates slink away on their small boats back to their villages, where they are paid some small piece of what the warlords make off with; and they wait until another ship comes along to do the whole thing again.

Except now, according to the briefings Felix had received, in some of the most dangerous waters on earth, the ship owners were growing tired of paying ransom, of having their ships hijacked, of the lawlessness of the pirates. The pirates were becoming more violent, too. They had started to shoot their hostages if payment didn't come quickly enough. They had started to funnel the money they made to terrorists in exchange for more weapons, better weapons, with which they could seize bigger ships and demand even more money.

The terrorist connection worried the US government.

Recently, a group of pirates had boarded a ship and shot the first mate in the foot, fleeing back to their pirate haven in Somali waters just as the navy arrived. They didn't get any ransom money, but they got away.

Something had to be done to stop the pirates from getting away again.

Several countries had come together to form the antipiracy task force and the USS *Ritland* was one of the ships the United States Navy had committed to the effort. It had been decided back in Washington, DC, that an example had to be made of would-be pirates.

The admirals had a plan: SEAL Team 6 would find the pirates' mother ship, from which they launched their latest raid, and would seize the ship and the pirates, to bring them back to face justice in a court of law. If they resisted arrest, the SEALs were authorized to use deadly force. By seizing a US cargo ship, the pirates had become enemy combatants to be captured or killed.

It was like the modern version of the old wanted posters: The pirates would be taken dead or alive.

■ ■ ■

"You and your sea lion are the first step in this operation," Lt. Commander Barcott told Felix as he stood in the command center on the USS *Ritland*, approximately half an hour away from intercepting the hijacked cargo ship. "Currently, there are six hijackers on board the cargo ship *Duchess*, and three more on board a small motorized skiff tied alongside, which is, we believe, their getaway vehicle. Reports tell us at least five of the hijackers, including the three on the skiff, are armed with AK-47 assault rifles. They have separated the captain of the *Duchess* and his first mate from the rest of the hostages and are holding them on board the skiff. Reports suggest that they are an experienced and confident pirate crew."

"Reports, sir?" Felix dared ask the Special Forces officer. "Where are these reports coming from?"

"One of the crew on board the *Duchess* was able to call the antipiracy task force and provide this information before the pirates shut off his communications," Lt. Commander Barcott explained. "Right now, that is our only source of information. Which is where you and Sly come in."

Felix tensed, ready and eager to get his orders. He pictured the sea lion, joyfully tossing the basketball, flashing his silly salute, guiding Felix out of his tank with his nose. All of it was play to him. But nine pirates armed with machine guns? That was hardly play.

Lt. Commander Barcott continued. "While we engage in standard negotiations with the hijackers, you will deploy your asset." The commander meant Sly, but Felix flinched. He hated to hear his aquatic partner called an "asset" like the sea lion was some kind of top secret torpedo. He was a living, breathing creature. "The asset will be responsible for attaching the tracking device to their skiff."

For a moment, Felix wondered why they couldn't just send navy scuba divers to attach the device, but he realized that the navy didn't want to risk putting American soldiers in harm's way, when they didn't know anything other than what the crew member of the *Duchess* had said on the phone. They didn't want to risk an incident. If the pirates saw a person in the water, they might shoot their hostages. They might shoot the person in the water, too. It wouldn't look good to have a Navy SEAL shot by a ragtag band of pirates. Felix guessed that someone way back in Washington, DC, who had never set foot on a navy warship, had made a decision: Rather than risk a human life, they could send a sea lion into the danger zone.

But that's what the Marine Mammal Program was for, thought Felix. A pang of doubt entered his mind: If a robot replaced Sly, then a sea lion wouldn't have to be put at risk, either. . . .

"We are certain they will take the captain and first mate as hostages after leaving the *Duchess*," Lt. Commander Barcott said. "We will follow the tracking signal to their mother ship, at which point Sly will place a listening device on the hull. After that, our teams will handle the rest."

Our teams. The SEALs.

Handle the rest. It was a much gentler thing to say than "we'll kill all the pirates," but that's what Lt. Commander Barcott really meant. SEALs were in the killing business after all.

Felix had to wonder if that meant he and Sly were in the killing business, too? He wanted to do good, to fight bad guys, but now that he was faced with the moment of doing it, he had his doubts.

Like a good sailor, he let none of his doubts show.

"Aye aye, sir," he said, giving the commander a crisp salute after he was dismissed. He returned to the boat, to Gutierrez and to Sly in his crate.

It didn't take long before they got the green light to put their boat in the water.

The mission was a "go" and the pirates' fates were sealed.

At least, it seemed that way at first, until everything went terribly, terribly wrong.

07:
THE ELEMENT OF
SURPRISE

THEY cut the waves in the dark, smashing into each rolling crest and bouncing to the next one. The front of their small boat stayed mostly out of the water as they sped along, and their engine's high-pitched whine seemed too loud to Felix.

"Don't worry!" Gutierrez shouted over at him. "The *Ritland* is deploying a helicopter over the *Duchess* to lower supplies to the pirates. They think it's part of the negotiation, but it's really so the noise of the chopper will drown out the sound of our engines. We can go as fast as we want."

Felix nodded. It seemed like the navy had thought of everything. All he had to do was get a little closer and send Sly into the water with the tracking device, just like in training.

When they were in position, Gutierrez cut the engines. Water slapped against the hull of their boat, splashing in, wetting the deck and their boots with the cool, salty ocean. The boat rolled gently with the sea swells, and in his crate, Sly nosed the wire front, anxious to get out. He might not know the particulars of their mission, but he had his harness on — black, not orange, now — so he was in uniform and knew it was time to work.

Felix opened the crate and Sly came bounding out on his flippers, his body bending as he walked, like a giant furry inchworm. It was easy to forget that Sly had a mouth full of very big, very strong teeth. Sly's friendliness, his long eyelashes and funny nubs for ears, his long, bristly whiskers and twitchy nose, made him sometimes seem like a neighborhood dog. But he was not a dog.

Sly was an ocean mammal, a hunter of fish and an intelligent, social creature. In the wild, sea lions hunted in packs, fought with rival groups and members of their own, and did their best to avoid falling prey to the sharks and killer whales that devoured sea lions whenever they could catch them. A neighborhood dog didn't have those concerns and didn't have the defenses against them. Sly was a lot of fun to work with, but he also commanded respect. If he chose to, he could hurt a person very badly.

Felix took the tracking device and held it out. Sly's neck stretched, his powerful jaws opened, and he clamped down on the specially designed handle. With a broad sweeping motion and a spoken command, Felix signaled Sly to place the beacon.

The sea lion hopped to the gunwale of the boat with the clamp in his mouth and dove into the water, hardly making a splash. In an instant, he was gone beneath the dark surface and Felix saw nothing but the ocean reflecting the moonlight. Looking up, he saw the moon itself hanging overhead, a bright silver disk, shining white stars spilling around it, and not a cloud in the sky. For this type of operation, a cloudy night would have been better. Even though they had no running lights, their small boat might still be visible on the ocean.

In the distance, he saw the running lights of the USS *Ritland*, and in the other direction, the hulking outline of the *Duchess*, dead in the water, its emergency lights the only illumination on deck. The helicopter had already peeled away to return to the *Ritland* now that Gutierrez had cut their boat engines. The pilot didn't want to stay close to the hijacked ship for too long, lest the pirates grow angry and take their anger out on their hostages.

Felix couldn't see the skiff tied to the side of the *Duchess*, but he knew that Sly would be able to see it. The navy employed sea lions because of their excellent vision underwater, even in the dark. Sly would have no problem finding what he was after. Felix just hoped that the little skiff was similar enough to the one they'd used in training.

If Sly put the beacon in the wrong place, or didn't place it at all, the whole mission would be in jeopardy. The navy intended to let the skiff get away with hostages on board. If they couldn't track it, a rescue mission would become a lot more dangerous. All Felix could do was hope this part went well.

In his mind, Felix imagined it going well. He pictured Sly's sleek body swimming through the dark, the pirates up above, standing on their boat, guns cradled in their arms while their hostages sat tied back-to-back in the center of the hull, frightened, waiting for rescue. The pirates perhaps spoke to one another, joked about what they would do with their ransom money when they got it, or perhaps they were silent, their eyes fixed on the USS *Ritland* in the distance, wondering what the navy might try. If they were professional pirates, and not just fishermen out to make a quick fortune, then they would be on high alert, ready to counter anything the US Navy would throw at them.

But they would never see Sly coming.

He would race up from the ocean, directly below the skiff, and his head would pop out just to the side of the boat, far enough from the engines so he wouldn't be injured if they turned on — that had been an important part of Sly's training — and then he would place the beacon by releasing the clamp in his mouth. It would attach to the side of the boat just below the waterline, where it would not be seen. To make sure it was firmly attached, Sly would tug it twice, just as he'd been taught to do, and if it came off, he would catch it in his jaws and try again. If it stayed on after those two tugs, Sly would turn around and swim back to the boat, his flippers propelling him so fast that very few animals in the wild could catch him. The sea lion's speed had developed over millions of years of evolution to help him evade sharks and killer whales, but now it would help him evade pirates.

Felix's daydream of the perfect mission was interrupted by the crack of gunfire in the night.

Their radio buzzed to life. "Shots fired! Shots fired!"

A spotlight on the *Duchess* flicked on and scanned the water. As it swept across the surface, Felix made out the shape of one of the pirates in the skiff firing his weapon. Felix's heart skipped a beat. He feared that Sly had been spotted and would be shot . . . but the pirate wasn't firing into the water. He was firing up into the air. He wasn't even aiming. The spotlight was moving wildly, rather than purposefully tracking a moving animal.

Felix turned to Gutierrez, who was wearing Night Optical Device goggles, or NODs, which let him see in the dark, casting everything in a ghoulish green light. He was watching the men in the skiff.

Felix wanted to ask him what he saw, but Lt. Commander Barcott beat him to it. "Give me a sitrep," his voice snapped over the radio. "Who has eyes on the hostages? Are the hostages in danger?"

"Negative," Gutierrez replied. "They're firing into the air."

"And our asset?" the radio crackled. "What is the status?"

Felix looked over the water again as the helicopter returned, its loud *whoosh* drowning out all other sounds. Even the gunfire couldn't be heard over its noise. The helicopter shined its own light onto the cargo ship, and the pirates on the deck shouted and waved their guns. They fired, but their shots were wild and wide of the helicopter.

"Permission to engage," the gunner requested over the radio.

"Negative! Hold your fire!" Lt. Commander Barcott ordered. "Do not engage. You do not have authorization to engage."

Felix feared that all the noise and chaos had spooked Sly. He was afraid the sea lion would be disoriented and get lost, swim the wrong direction, lose his way.

But Sly was in his element and was not so easily startled. He popped up in the dark water near the exact spot where Felix was standing. His bright black eyes shined and he let out a high, sharp bark.

"Aoof! Aoof!"

Felix motioned for Sly to jump on board and get in his crate. He tossed him a fish as Gutierrez radioed back.

"Asset is on board and he has delivered the package," he said.

"Affirmative," Lt. Commander Barcott replied. "Come back to Kermit."

Kermit was the code name for the USS *Ritland*. Gutierrez didn't hesitate to swing the boat around and gun the engines.

As they sped back, content that they had done their part of the mission, the shooting had stopped. The *Duchess*'s spotlight cut off and the helicopter shut its light off, too, banking to the left as it began its flight back to "Kermit."

"What do you think all that was about?" Gutierrez asked Felix as they drove back.

Felix shrugged. "Maybe the pirates just wanted to remind us they were armed and dangerous."

"It doesn't add up," Gutierrez said, shaking his head. "If they didn't see Sly, why'd they start shooting? Why'd they turn the light on? Just to get our attention?"

Felix wondered. They certainly had gotten everyone's attention. The helicopter had returned. Everyone on the *Ritland* had probably been glued to their radios or their binoculars, wondering what the shooting was all about, wondering if the hostages were okay. It was like the pirates wanted everyone in the area looking right at them. Why would they want that? Wouldn't the criminals want to avoid attention from a warship like the *Ritland* as much as possible?

Unless they were trying to create a distraction, Felix thought.

As if answering his unspoken thought, at the same moment, the pirates' plan revealed itself.

A huge blast erupted from the waterline on the starboard side of the USS *Ritland*'s hull, a ball of fire shooting a hundred feet into the air. The bone-shaking bang took a moment longer to travel across the water, and the shock wave forced the small boat with Felix, Gutierrez, and Sly to turn off course. A cloud of black smoke blotted out the silver moon. Sirens blared.

"What the — ?" Gutierrez gasped.

"A bomb!" Felix replied. "They distracted us while they planted a bomb!"

The radio crackled again, but they couldn't make out any words. Already they could see the USS *Ritland* listing to the side as the burning ship took on water and slowly began to sink. In the light of the flames, Felix could see sailors in the water, some of them swimming, some of them still.

The engines on board the hijacked cargo ship suddenly roared to life. Rather than coming to the rescue, it started to move away from the scene, full speed ahead. The pirates were getting away and the *Ritland* was going down.

Gutierrez accelerated toward the burning warship, where the rest of the sea lion team and 189 other souls were suddenly in grave peril.

Felix and Gutierrez had a new mission now: search and rescue.

08:
SURVIVORS

FELIX wasn't exactly sure what they should do, but both he and Gutierrez had received basic emergency medic's training. They could bandage wounds, tie tourniquets to stop serious bleeding, treat less severe burns, and perform CPR. Their boat could also hold about eight people, so they could at least get a few sailors out of the water to tend to their wounds.

As they drew closer and saw the scale of the explosion, the giant hole it had ripped in the side of the ship, they knew their small boat would hardly be enough for all the casualties they would encounter. There had been nearly two hundred people on board the USS *Ritland*, and it looked like most of them would need help.

The helicopter had been in flight when the explosion happened, so it was safe in the air above, as long as its fuel held out. It shined its spotlight into the water, and what Felix saw stopped his breath in his throat.

The ocean was littered with debris. Their rigid-hull inflatable boat was still a hundred yards out from the ship and already they had to slow their engines to avoid crashing into shrapnel torn from the steel hull.

At fifty yards out, they saw the first bodies, charred remains of what had once been men and women of the United States Navy. The bodies farthest from the ship had been in the blast radius of the explosion and they were burned black as coal. Some bobbed like tops in the water, upside down; some floated still as store mannequins, their scorched faces staring straight into the night sky, far beyond hope of seeing anything through lifeless eyes. There was nothing Felix or Gutierrez could do for them. The air smelled of chemicals and smoke, burning flesh and fuel. Patches of oil flamed on the surface of the ocean, like the water itself was on fire, like the whole world and all the laws of nature had been blown apart with the blast that ripped apart the USS *Ritland*.

"A sneak attack. The scumbags," Gutierrez muttered, too shocked to even use the curse words that might have otherwise flowed naturally from his mouth. Sailors were not known for their prim and proper speech after all. But now, the act of cursing seemed wrong in the face of such a sudden and brutal attack. Even Sly in his crate was still and silent with a wide-eyed look on his face. He couldn't possibly understand what had happened, but he looked very aware that something was wrong.

Gutierrez stopped their engines so they could listen. Voices cried out from the water — the voices of those who still could cry out.

"There!" Felix pointed to movement on the surface. Gutierrez guided the boat and the helicopter above shined its light ahead of them, illuminating a swimmer in the water. He was holding a fellow sailor in one arm and using his other to swim toward them. When they drew close enough, the man in the water thrust up the figure he was holding and Felix hauled the body on board. It was a woman, and she was badly burned.

At first, Felix didn't recognize her, but then he saw the insignia on her uniform. He looked down at the man in the water and recognized him as the veterinary assistant. The woman in Felix's arms was Sly's veterinarian, Dr. Morris. He laid her in the hull as Gutierrez helped her assistant on board. She was breathing, and her heartbeat was steady. Her burns weren't good, but they wouldn't be fatal if she got medical attention soon.

"A Mayday call has gone out," Felix told the assistant, who had a cut on his forehead that had already begun to clot. The man nodded. His eyes were glassy, unfocused. Felix feared he had a concussion. "Help is on the way, but it'll be a few hours. You stay awake, okay? Dr. Morris needs you."

The man nodded again.

Felix realized the bomb must have gone off very near the sea lion team's cargo hold. If he and Sly had been on board, they would surely have been blown apart in the explosion. Sly's dangerous mission had actually saved their lives.

The boat continued its slow patrol along the wounded ship's hull. The *Ritland* was sinking lower in the water. The helicopter had to pull up. The wind from its rotors was churning the ocean and pushing the bodies away. Over the roar of its noise, Felix couldn't hear the cries for help coming from the water around them.

They found two more sailors alive, not from their sea lion team. They were enlisted men, caught down below by the blast. On deck, Felix could see men and woman scurrying about, tending to the wounded as best they could, loading them into boats to get them away from the choking black smoke. Felix wished they could coordinate over the radio, but it seemed the blast had damaged communications systems. Regardless, anyone well enough to talk on the radio was busy trying to help the casualties around them.

After twenty minutes, the small boat had only four survivors of the explosion on board. Everyone else they had found was already dead.

Felix knew it would be hours before rescue ships from the task force arrived. The ocean was vast, and the distance between the *Ritland* and the nearest ship was hundreds of miles. He tried not to think about the terrorist pirates on board the *Duchess* getting away, using the time to race back to their port in Somalia, where they could escape justice.

Or where they *thought* they could escape justice. Sly had tagged their skiff. The navy was probably already tracking them via satellite. There would be time to go after them. For now, Felix had to focus on the problem at hand. There were still a lot of sailors trapped inside the burning ship, and the lower it sank in the water, the more difficult it would be to rescue them.

More difficult for people to rescue them, he thought. *Not for Sly.*

He looked to the sea lion in his crate, whose whiskers

twitched as he smelled the acrid air and blood and burning. His acute hearing would separate the sounds of groaning metal from the sounds of groaning men.

"Take the boat closer to the blast site," Felix said.

"Are you crazy?" Gutierrez replied. "She's going down, and the force of water she's pulling with her could suck us under, too. We have to get some distance with the survivors."

"There are more survivors to rescue," Felix said. "Sly can do it."

In addition to attaching beacons, Sly was trained to locate swimmers in the water, like he had at Naval Base Point Loma in San Diego for years. They had the clamp and towline equipment on board their little boat right now. Gutierrez looked at Felix and then looked at Sly in his crate.

"Fine," he sighed and took the boat in closer. Felix was glad Gutierrez was the kind of guy who would always do the right thing, even if he was also the kind of guy who always grumbled about it.

The hole in the side of the warship was three decks

high. Wires and metal hung loose from the gaps and tears. Someone had thought to cut off power, so the wires that dangled into the water weren't charged with electricity. *Good thing*, Felix thought. Electricity and water don't mix well. Or rather, they mix far too well. If Sly brushed against a live wire in the wreckage, he'd be fried in an instant. The lack of sparks in the wreck was a relief.

It was the only relief Felix saw.

They drifted closer until they were nearly inside the flooded hull and could see the whole grisly scene: the cargo hold in shambles, control rooms blasted open, bodies slumped over where they'd fallen, either tossed there by the explosion, burned and broken, or perished from smoke inhalation as they tried to rescue their shipmates. Below the waterline, Felix saw the top of an access door, blasted apart. Beyond it, he knew, was the hallway down to the mess, where the enlisted sailors ate their meals. In his short time on board, Felix hadn't gotten to know the ship very well, but he could remember the places he'd been: his billet where he slept, the mess where he ate, the command center where Lt. Commander Barcott and Lieutenant Greff had given him the orders that saved his life. He hoped there were survivors in each of those places.

Felix helped the wounded to clear a spot on the deck of the small boat in front of Sly's crate. He opened it and gestured for Sly to come out.

Sly hesitated. His head swung from side to side. He was saying no. He hadn't been taught to shake his head, but he'd spent so much time around humans, he'd begun mimicking some of their behaviors. It had amused the trainers back in San Diego, so they never discouraged it. Felix had never really thought that Sly knew what the high five or the head shake meant. It seemed, however, that he did. Sly backed up in his crate, scrunching his six-hundred-pound body into a clump in the corner.

"Come on, Sly," Felix urged in his sweetest voice, repeating the gesture to call Sly out of his crate. "We're gonna do some good."

Sly didn't move. Sea lions did not survive in the wild by ignoring their instincts when they sensed death and danger. Sly sensed plenty of both.

Felix crouched down to Sly's eye level, looked at him through the crate. The black eyes were wide with fear, the thick whiskers pointed back over his snout. He shivered through his whole body. The night air was cool, but Sly's fur kept him comfortable even in arctic waters. He would not be shivering from cold here in the Arabian Sea. Sly was shivering from terror.

Felix wanted to comfort his friend. But he also wanted to get him out of the crate to save some lives. He crawled forward on his hands and knees, poking himself into the crate, and he reached out his hand to pat Sly.

He should have known better.

Sly was not his friend. Sly was a wild animal, afraid.

The sea lion's lips curled and his large teeth flashed, his powerful neck bent, and with the speed of a cobra, he lashed out, snapping his jaws at Felix's out-stretched arm.

"Ah!" Felix jumped back, grazed by the bite. A second later, blood poured from his forearm where one of Sly's teeth had caught him. Felix cradled the arm, applied pressure to the wound, and tried to calm his racing heart.

Sly, immediately sensing he'd done something wrong, laid himself flat on the bottom of his crate and rolled to his side, exposing his belly. He had made himself vulnerable. A sea lion's natural instinct when winning a fight would have been to continue to establish his dominance, to show no weakness. Sly, stuck between the sea lion world and the human world, had attacked like a sea lion, but was now apologizing like a person.

Felix did what they always did in training. He ignored the bad behavior. He let the moment pass, even as he tore the sleeve from his shirt to use as a bandage. The real bandages on board were sterile, and he was saving the few they had for the burn victims, who were very vulnerable to infection.

He repeated the gesture for Sly to come out of the crate.

Sly, submissive now, hesitated.

Felix repeated it once more, and this time, Sly obeyed. He lifted himself from the floor of his crate and shimmied to the door.

The men on deck tensed as he came out. They'd just seen his wild side and they feared it. Felix did not fear it. He understood it. He had to be careful, and respectful, but he did not have to be afraid.

He tossed Sly a fish and praised him for coming out, then he gave him the leg clamp and the instruction to locate a swimmer in the water. Sly understood and dove from the boat.

He trusted Felix, and Felix trusted him. They would let no real harm come to each other. They would do their jobs. If Sly found someone, he would attach the clamp. Then he'd come back and signal to Felix that he'd been successful. Felix knew they couldn't haul survivors out with the winch; that would be too dangerous through the dark and winding passages of the sinking ship, but they had scuba gear on board, an air tank and flippers and a mask. It was a small tank, but it would be enough. Felix would dive down and follow the line. He could reach the survivor, assess the situation, and lead the person back out carefully.

The thought actually cheered him up. He wouldn't be sending his obedient partner to do all the dangerous work alone. He was going to do some of it himself, even with his injured arm. They were a team after all, and they'd share the risks together.

Half an hour had passed since the explosion.

Felix prayed there would still be survivors belowdecks for them to find.

09:
SEAL HUGS

FELIX peered through the broken hull of the ship from the relative safety of the inflatable boat. He saw Sly's head pop up for a breath in a narrow space deep inside the *Ritland*. A patch of oil burned with bright blue heat on the water just beside the sea lion's small brown head, but now that Sly had a task, he wasn't frightened. A jet of air shot from his nostrils and then he dove again, the clamp still clutched in his mouth, the line unspooling from the RHIB's winch.

Minutes passed. The hull creaked and groaned. A small, swirling whirlpool appeared nearby as water flowed into an air pocket that had collapsed somewhere below. Felix hoped there were no sailors trapped down there. He hoped he hadn't sent Sly in to get trapped.

"She's sinking faster," Gutierrez said. "We can't stay here too much longer. We need to get to a safe distance."

Felix ignored him. He was right, of course. They couldn't risk the lives of all the people they'd already rescued, but they also couldn't abandon any sailors still trapped below. It was an impossible choice, but one he knew every man and woman on board their small boat would agree on: They'd stay as long as they could and save as many of the crew as possible. That was their duty to their shipmates, to their countrymen — to their fellow human beings. Gutierrez understood that, too, and said no more about leaving. Felix nodded his thanks.

A minute later, the line Sly was pulling stopped unspooling. It grew taut and then jiggled once. Then again. That was Sly testing that it was firmly attached, like he'd been trained.

"We've got someone!" Felix cheered. He hoisted the oxygen tank onto his back and strapped his feet into the flippers. He kept his mask hanging around his neck and the breathing hose and regulator in his right hand. He strapped an underwater flashlight to his wrist and checked to make sure it worked. Then he waited. He wouldn't jump in himself until Sly was safely returned.

Luckily, Sly came back just as they'd practiced, hopping aboard with a wet splash. His body glistened, slick from all the spilled oil and other chemicals leaking from the ship. Felix hadn't even considered that he'd sent Sly into such polluted water. He glanced at Dr. Morris, still unconscious. He felt bad, like he'd broken his promise to keep Sly out of danger. He also wished she were awake so that she could check Sly out, make sure the pollution in the water hadn't hurt him.

He tossed Sly a fish and let him go back into his crate, where he felt safe, so he could rest until Felix came back with the sailor he'd found and they could reset the clamp and do it again.

"My turn," he said. He pulled his mask over his face, popped the breathing apparatus into his mouth, and jumped into the filthy water. He gave a thumbs-up to the boat to show he was okay, then he grabbed the towline with one hand and began to make his way down, following it underwater into the depths of the ship.

His flashlight made a bright cone of white in the dark. He swept it slowly from side to side in front of him, like a blind man tapping his walking stick on the sidewalk to avoid running into obstacles. He kept his right hand wrapped around the line so he didn't get lost.

He soon found himself at the passage that led into the heart of the ship. The door was blown away and the line twisted through the opening. With the light swinging in front of him, he turned the corner and ran smack into the grinning face of a dead man, white teeth shining where the skin had been torn away from the skull.

Felix screamed with shock. A flood of bubbles escaped his mouth. He let go of the line and kicked back, pulling himself away from the gruesome sight.

He was soon back in the cargo hold, trying to calm his breathing, telling himself not to panic. The dead couldn't hurt him. Whoever was still alive down below was running out of time. He had to press on in spite of his fear. Fear was good, he told himself. Fear would keep him focused. There could be no bravery without fear. He let himself feel afraid, and swam forward anyway.

He found the line once more, reaching out to clutch it in his fingers. He took one slow breath, letting the bubbles tickle his ears as he exhaled, focusing on that tickle, the real feelings of water and air in the dark, not the imaginary feelings of terror that his mind created. He turned the corner to meet the floating body face-to-face once more.

He did not turn away this time. He shined the light directly ahead. And despite the terrible wounds, he recognized the man. It was Lieutenant Greff.

Felix wished he'd known him better. He knew his commanding officer had been a serious man with a serious commitment to service and duty. He didn't know if Lieutenant Greff had had a family, or what he had done for fun, or who would be waiting with bated breath for a call to learn if he was okay or not. That call would break someone's heart.

Felix was sorry the man had died and was sorry he'd recoiled from his body. He crossed himself as he'd done in Catholic school as a boy, and then he gently pushed the body aside. He swam past.

He passed three more corpses floating in the hallway before he reached the next turn. They looked peaceful suspended in the water. Felix didn't recognize any of the others, but still he crossed himself as he passed, thinking the only thought that seemed right. It wasn't a prayer. It was a simple *I'm sorry this happened to you*.

The line led him to a stairwell. The door to the stairs should have been closed tight to stop the ship from flooding, but the explosion must have caused the system to fail. He swam through the door and followed the line up the stairs, swimming where once he'd walked. Loose garbage floated like jellyfish, and the bubbles from his breathing knocked the trash about.

He kicked along the line down another passage, one that looked familiar even though it was tilted sideways. He knew that he would turn another corner and be at the door to the command center.

Just then, the whole ship shuddered and the water around him seemed to squeal. Something had shifted, something had broken. The angle of the hallway grew steeper. The ship was sinking faster. He kicked onward until the line led him to the command center door.

It, too, was open, but not because it was damaged. It looked like it had been opened so that the officers inside could get out. He also saw as he exhaled that his bubbles broke on the surface of the water above, meaning there was an air pocket. The command center wasn't completely underwater.

He followed the line up and came into water where he could stand. It only came to his waist, and when he stood and took the regulator from his mouth and pulled the mask down around his neck, he saw that Sly's line went beneath a console that had collapsed. There were two men pinned beneath that console, one of whom Felix recognized as Lt. Commander Barcott of Navy SEAL Team Six. He was hunched over, his chin just above the waterline. The second man floated at an awkward angle, facedown in the water. Felix knew immediately he was dead.

"I need your help getting this off the commander," another man said. He appeared uninjured and remarkably calm. Both his hands rested on the fallen console. "His leg is stuck under here."

"Where is everyone else?" Felix asked.

"I ordered them to evacuate," Lt. Commander Barcott said through gritted teeth. He was in a good deal of pain, but doing his best to fight through it. "Lieutenant Coyle here disobeyed my orders."

"You can put a reprimand in my file, sir," Coyle said. "Once we get you out of here."

Felix made his way across the room.

"Your sea lion put a clamp on my leg," Barcott said. "We didn't know what he was up to. He just showed up in here, attached that thing to me, and swam away."

"Just doing his job, sir," said Felix. "And we're gonna do ours now."

He grabbed one side of the console and the guy named Coyle grabbed the other. They bent from the knees and hoisted with all their strength.

It barely moved.

"Argh!" Barcott grunted. Even the smallest movement caused him agony. "The ship is sinking and you boys need to get out of here now."

"Negative, sir," Coyle repeated. He nodded to Felix and they tried again.

Still the console barely moved. Felix could feel the ship shuddering beneath him. His eyes met Coyle's. The man was not going to leave his commander. That was not how SEALs operated. The water was cloudy with blood, and if the commander didn't get medical attention soon, he would be added to the list of the dead.

"This is a direct order, sailors," Lt. Commander Barcott snapped at them. "You will evacuate immediately. You will not give two more victims to the terrorists who did this."

"A SEAL does not leave a man behind," Coyle told his commander, and just as Lt. Commander Barcott was about to argue, something burst through the surface of the water: a big brown head, with long whiskers and bright black eyes.

"Sly!" Felix called out, surprised. The sea lion had come for him.

Suddenly, Lt. Commander Barcott burst out laughing. His pale lips pulled back, his teeth shined in the dark. He laughed so hard he winced. Felix feared the commander had just lost his mind.

"A SEAL doesn't leave a man behind!" Barcott repeated, cackling. "A seal? Get it? Ha-ha!"

"Puns? You're making puns now?" Coyle shook his head. He laughed, too. Then he turned to Felix. "Can your sea lion help us?"

"He can," said Felix. Sly was certainly strong enough to move the console. "But I don't know if he will. We've never trained to do anything like this . . . but there's only one way to find out."

Felix signaled Sly to come near. The sea lion did and he patted Sly's side to keep him calm. Then he and Coyle grabbed the console again and heaved.

At first, Sly just watched. Felix had seen the animal imitate a high five and salute. He'd seen him bark and sing along with the radio. If he could mimic people in all those things, Felix hoped, he could mimic them now.

"Come on come on come on," Felix muttered as he put all his strength into lifting the console up.

Sly moved forward, dove below the surface, and disappeared into the dark water. Felix's heart sank a moment until, suddenly, they felt the console rise up from below, like it was floating. He saw in the water that Sly had swum under it and used all his strength as a swimmer to push it up with his tough nose.

"Grab the commander!" Felix called out.

Coyle grabbed Lt. Commander Barcott roughly by the collar and dragged him out from underneath the console as fast as he could. The commander screamed with pain, but he was free. Sly let the console fall again, and swam back up to the surface with a triumphant "Aoof!"

Felix didn't even think about the wound on his arm that Sly had given him less than twenty minutes earlier. He bent down in the water and wrapped the giant furry beast in a hug. Sly responded by wrapping his front flipper around Felix's waist.

Felix would never think of it as a bear hug again. From now on, when he wanted to show his appreciation, he'd be giving seal hugs.

10:
ABANDON SHIP

THE ship shuddered. From somewhere in its hull, they heard the screech of snapping metal. It was time to go.

"How are we getting out of here?" Coyle asked, interrupting the hug between the sea lion and his trainer.

"We'll follow the line on the commander's ankle," said Felix. "The other end is on our boat. We'll have to swim for it. Can you do that, Commander?"

Barcott nodded. "We're SEALs," he said. "This is like a walk in the park."

"It's underwater for a while," Felix explained. "So we'll have to share this one tank I've got. Three breaths, then pass the mouthpiece to the next guy. Three breaths, then pass. We'll make it out that way."

He signaled Sly to go back to the boat and Sly, happy to recognize a command he'd actually trained on, dove out of sight.

Felix gave Commander Barcott the regulator to breathe through first. He and Lieutentant Coyle took deep breaths and they ducked underwater together. The three of them made their way through the submerged doorway and into the dark corridors below.

After the commander took three breaths, he gave the regulator to Felix by shoving the mouthpiece directly into his face. Felix bit down on it, exhaled to clear the water out, and took his three breaths, swimming forward all the while. The last breath he took was a deep one, then he shoved the mouthpiece at Coyle. Coyle took his three breaths and passed it back to the commander. It went like that as they swam back down the stairwell and along the hallway where the bodies floated and through the flooded cargo hold, and then they burst to the surface, where the fires still burned on the oil and the small boat still floated just beyond the hole in the ship.

"You okay?" Gutierrez called out the moment he saw them.

Felix gave a thumbs-up. He saw Sly swimming circles around the boat, waiting for the slow humans to catch up. The moment they started forward, Sly swam over to Felix and started bumping him with his nose, like he was nudging him to hurry.

When they were all on board, Gutierrez started the engines and steered away from the sinking ship.

"We can find more survivors!" Felix called out over the engines.

"No time," Gutierrez replied. "Ship's going down and we've got to get these casualties to the medical station on board the USS *Henderson*. It's the nearest ship."

As they sped off, Felix looked back over his shoulder at the USS *Ritland*, foundering. The sun was just peeking red over the horizon and the ship was cast in silhouette on the water. Felix gave Sly a fish and sent him to rest in his crate while he treated the lieutenant commander's wounds to the best of his ability.

There were still men in the ocean, swimming back and forth to help the ones who couldn't swim anymore. There were lifeboats and rescue boats that had come off the *Ritland* itself, moving through the chaos, picking sailors up, tending to their wounds. There was activity all around. The sailors were helping one another and would keep helping one another until the moment the rescue ships arrived. For now, Felix and Sly couldn't help any more of them. Their boat was full and they had to get the men and women they'd saved to an infirmary as fast as they could.

As they sped away, Felix wondered where the pirates were at the moment. Had the *Duchess* with its hostages reached a pirates' port yet? And where was the small skiff with the tracking device attached? Had they separated or stayed by the side of the big cargo ship?

Felix was tired and he was frightened and he was angry and he was sad for all the lives that had been lost that night, and all his muscles ached, and it felt like it took all his energy just to keep his eyes open, but still, just then, he smiled.

The pirates had no idea that Sly had attached that device to their little boat. Wherever they went, the US Navy would find them. He and Sly had made sure of that.

The pirates would be brought to justice for what they'd done, Felix told himself. Dead or alive.

11:
AFTERMATH

BY the time they reached the USS *Henderson*, the Marine Corps Fleet Antiterrorism Security Team had arrived. Those marines, known as FAST company, had flown in to secure the area around the sinking ship and to guard the rescue ships from further attacks. They wore the patches of their unit on their sleeves and Felix took note of their motto: "Anytime, anyplace." Joining them on board the *Henderson* and preparing for action were marines from the Recapture Tactics Team, who were like the SWAT team on a local police force.

The rigid-hull inflatable boat was loaded up a launch ramp. As Felix led Sly out of his crate and on board the ship, the navy corpsmen tended to the wounded, rushing them to the infirmary, and leaving Sly, Felix, and Gutierrez to themselves again.

There was no designated area for the sea lion, so Felix and Gutierrez penned off a part of the forward deck, somewhere they thought might be out of the way, and they kept Sly in his crate there. Felix knew it would be a while before they could get a properly equipped helicopter to take them back to port in Bahrain. For the time being, all available aircraft would be needed for more important things.

Lt. Commander Barcott was just one of the casualties who would be flown out to a military hospital in Germany for surgery. According to a corpsman Felix asked, the man had lost a lot of blood, and he had a long road to recovery ahead of him.

As a helicopter landed to take the lieutenant commander away, his SEAL teammate, Lieutenant Coyle, found Felix on deck. There were twenty other members of the SEAL teams with him, out of the twenty-four who'd come on board the USS *Ritland* to begin with.

"We wanted to thank you," Coyle said. "And Sly. For coming back for Commander Barcott. You saved his life."

"He'd have done the same for me," Felix said, although in his head he thought how amazing it was that nearly a whole Navy SEAL troop was thanking him for his actions on his first overseas deployment. It wasn't something he'd planned or even hoped for, but he was proud to have done some good on this mission.

"You should know, we've got your back from now on, whenever we can," Coyle told him. "The teams" — he used the casual shorthand for Navy SEAL teams — "don't forget a friend. If we can ever do anything for you, or your partner there, let us know. We're happy to help a fellow seal."

Felix chuckled again at the seal-SEAL joke. In his crate, Sly was sleeping soundly, tired from the effort of the night. A sea lion put out energy in short bursts and needed lots of rest in between. He wouldn't be up and about for hours.

"I'll let him know when he wakes up," said Felix.

"Give him an extra fish from us," Coyle said.

"Aye aye," Felix replied.

One by one, the surviving men of the SEAL team shook his hand, then went back to see off their commanding officer.

"Hey!" Felix called out as the last of them were walking away.

"Yeah?" Coyle turned around to him.

Felix could have asked the guy anything. He could have asked him to write a report about how amazing the sea lion team was, how the Marine Mammal Program should never be shut down, how they saved lives. But he wasn't worried about saving his job right now. Instead, he asked: "What about the guys who did this? Is there a counterattack planned?"

"Technically, that's classified information," Coyle said, but then he nodded. "But you bet there is a counterattack planned. Nobody gets to do this to us and get away with it."

"Will your team be — ?" Felix started.

"We will be involved in the operation," said Coyle. "Yes."

Felix swallowed hard. He didn't really know how to ask what he wanted. "If there's a role for us . . . for Sly . . . well . . . we want to help."

Coyle's face broke into a smile. "Request noted," Coyle said.

When he'd gone, Gutierrez sidled up to Felix. "You crazy?" he asked. "You think we can keep up with those guys on a combat mission?"

Felix shrugged. "If we can help, then we should help."

"The navy's not gonna send us along," Gutierrez said. "They've got procedures and plans and all that. We'll be ordered back to San Diego and we'll watch this play out on the news. We're not a combat team."

"I think Lieutenant Coyle's as good as his word. If there's a role for us in the mission, then they'll include us."

"But why do you *want* to be included?" Gutierrez

threw his arms in the air. "You want . . . what? Revenge?"

"On the pirates who bombed our ship and killed our people? Don't you?" Felix asked.

Gutierrez just shook his head sadly.

Felix sighed. "It's more than that," he continued. He remembered his promise to Commander Jackson. He'd told her he wouldn't say anything about the Marine Mammal Program closing. But he needed Gutierrez to understand why he was suddenly willing to take such risks.

"We're being shut down," he said. "This deployment is our last chance to prove to the top brass that the program is worth keeping. If we can demonstrate our usefulness in the war on terrorists . . . well, maybe they'll keep the Marine Mammal Program open."

Gutierrez's mouth hung slack. "They're shutting us down?"

Felix nodded. "We're going to be reassigned. Sly, too."

Felix felt his voice catch in his throat. The reality of it all suddenly hit him. If the program was shut down after this mission, he and Sly would be separated. He might never see his sea lion again.

Gutierrez sighed. He put his hand on Felix's shoulder. He didn't exactly say he was okay with Felix's idea, but he didn't argue with it, either.

"I'm exhausted," he said. "We should do like Sly and get some rest."

There was no room belowdecks for them and the morning air was warm. It would be blazing hot on deck soon and they would have to work hard to keep Sly cool and comfortable, so they just lay down beside the equipment and coolers of fish they'd brought on board — all that was left of the sea lion team's supplies — and took a nap. Felix rested his head on his hands and stared straight up at the morning sky. All around him there was noise and motion: men and women rushing about to help the wounded, helicopters hovering for their turn to land on the back of the ship, personnel arriving, casualties leaving.

It was a wonder anyone would ever be able to rest in such a din, but Sly slept soundly in his crate. In nature, a pod of sea lions could number in the thousands. When they gathered to sun on the rocks, to sleep and socialize, the sounds of snores and barks and roars could rival the noise of an entire city. Sea lions had adapted to sleep through just about any cacophony.

Guys in the navy quickly learned to do the same, as sailors could be nearly as loud as a pod of wild sea mammals. In minutes, Felix was asleep.

He dreamed of fire and danger. Over and over, his mind conjured the explosion at sea. In his dream, he was swimming beside Sly in the ocean when the bombs exploded and Sly swam into the fire. No matter how fast Felix swam, he could not catch up. His partner was in danger. His ship was sinking. His country had been attacked. And yet he couldn't swim fast enough to help. He clawed at the water, kicking and splashing, but with every sweeping stroke of his arms, Sly got farther and farther away. As Sly's brown head popped up for air, he turned to look back at Felix and called out, "Felix! Felix!"

Felix woke from his dream with a start, sweating. The sun was up, a bright blazing ball of fire hanging in a cloudless sky.

"Felix!" he heard again. For a confused moment he still believed it was Sly speaking to him, but his mind followed him into wakefulness and his eyes focused. Gutierrez had squatted down beside him, had his hand on Felix's shoulder, was shaking him awake. "Looks like you've got your wish. Lieutenant Coyle's requested us for a briefing."

"Uh," was all Felix could muster. His lips were parched and his throat dry. Gutierrez handed him a bottle of water. He sat up and saw that they'd been joined by five other members of the sea lion support team. Probably all that was left. One of them had a hose and was running cool water over Sly's back. The sea lion was out of his crate, rolling under the stream of water and howling with delight.

"We've got ten minutes," said Gutierrez. "I thought I'd let you rest as long as I could. My guess is you're gonna need it." Felix nodded his thanks and stood, still shaken from his dream and from the harrowing events of the night. "By the way," Gutierrez added, "the lieutenant told me the SEALs use their own boat drivers, SWCC guys."

"SWCC?" Felix wondered.

"Special Warfare Combat Crewmen," he explained. "They insert and extract the SEALs."

"Oh," Felix said, looking down. He couldn't imagine going on a mission without Gutierrez driving, but his friend hadn't really wanted to go into combat anyway, so it was probably a good thing the SEALs had their own drivers.

"So I told him that I'm not just a driver," Gutierrez said. "I'm a member of the Mark Six sea lion team in the Navy Marine Mammal Program, and as long as the program is around, I go where you and Sly go. No matter what."

Felix met his eyes. He smiled and Gutierrez smiled back.

"No matter what?" Felix asked.

"No matter what," Gutierrez repeated. "Now let's go to this briefing. I feel like capturing some pirates today."

12:
WARRIORS

THEY were worried about underwater mines.

"A British naval destroyer, the HMS *Potter*, intercepted the hijacked cargo ship before it could reach port," Lieutenant Coyle told the assembled Navy SEALs, SWCC boat captains, marines, and the two members of the Marine Mammal Program, Felix and Gutierrez. "A British strike force has boarded and recovered most of the hostages, and captured three of the pirates. The rest escaped on board the small skiff, which we were able to track thanks to the Mark Six sea lion team."

All heads in the room swiveled around to Felix. Everyone had dark circles under their eyes, but their jaws were hard and set and their faces showed them ready for action. They gave Felix and Gutierrez appreciative nods and turned back to the briefing. Felix was very aware that he and Gutierrez were the only guys in the room who weren't trained and experienced "trigger pullers."

"The pirates still have two hostages. Their skiff has fled into this bay, here." The lieutenant pointed at a map on a large screen that took up one whole wall of the briefing room. "This is a known pirate haven controlled by the warlord who goes by the name Surfer Boy."

"Surfer Boy?" one of the SEALs asked.

A picture appeared on the screen of the pirate warlord, dressed in combat fatigues, with wraparound sunglasses on his face. He wore a shell necklace and his short hair was dyed bright blond, an unheard-of color for a Somali person. The men in the room muttered.

"He has been known to play Beach Boys albums as he raids villages and attacks ships," Lieutenant Coyle explained. "He is also known to have ties to various terrorist networks throughout Africa and the Middle East. We believe he is responsible for organizing at least one third of all pirate attacks in this region in the past three years. And thanks to the pirates we captured, we now know he was behind the bombing last night. He lured the USS *Ritland* there, even made sure that the cargo ship's first mate radioed us. He planned that attack from beginning to end and we fell right into his trap. We'd like to spring a trap of our own, tonight, while we still know his location."

"Oorah," one of the marines in the room grunted, which was the marine corps' battle cry. It was met with a quick and loud "Hooyah!" which was the Navy SEALs' battle cry. Lieutenant Coyle raised his hand up for silence, which was a relief to Felix, because as far as he knew, the Marine Mammal Program didn't have a battle cry. They'd never gone into battle before. He was tempted to bark like Sly, but he wondered if anyone would even recognize a sea lion bark. It didn't really matter. The moment had passed.

Lieutenant Coyle started speaking directly to Felix: "We'll send in the sea lion team on a RHIB with two SEALs on board. The sea lion — whose name, by the way, is Sly" — he smiled at Felix, glad to have remembered the sea lion's name — "will be deployed to locate and mark any underwater explosives that have been planted in the bay. Two squads from DEVGRU" — he meant SEAL Team Six — "will land on the beach, locate the captain and first mate of the *Duchess*, and effect their rescue by any means necessary. When the hostages are clear on the boats, the marines will insert on the beach for Phase Two." He pointed to a satellite picture of a small group of buildings at the top of a ridge of sand dunes overlooking the beach. "The marines will secure the area, search the buildings, and capture or kill Surfer Boy. All units will then return to the boats using the marked route, and rendezvous again with the *Henderson* on the edge of Somali territorial waters. Questions?"

"Rules of engagement, sir?" one of the SEALs asked.

"Deadly force is authorized to maintain mission secrecy," the lieutenant said. "Otherwise, defensive action only."

The guys shifted in their seats. They knew they were going into a hostile area, but the rules seemed kind of vague. They could shoot in order to "maintain mission secrecy," like if a guard spotted them and was going to raise the alarm, but in any other circumstance they could only shoot in self-defense. It was confusing, and would be more confusing when they were in the thick of danger.

Lieutenant Coyle obviously wanted to keep the men focused. "Listen, we'll do what we need to get the job done. These guys threw the first punch, gentlemen, but we throw the knockout punch, understood?"

"Aye aye, sir," the room shouted with one voice. Felix and Gutierrez shouted, too, caught up in the moment. The briefing room felt like a high school locker room before a big game. It even smelled like one.

"We go at nineteen hundred. Make ready," Lieutenant Coyle said, then dismissed them to prepare.

In the hallway, two of the SEALs caught up with Felix and Gutierrez and introduced themselves by their last names, Adams and McNamara. They were going to be in the boat with Sly on this mission, armed and ready to defend the sea lion and his handler with lethal force. Sly had never had bodyguards before. Neither had Felix.

"You focus on your job and we'll get you guys out of that pirate bay safe and sound," the one named Adams said. He was a broad-shouldered guy, with a scar across his neck.

The SWCC driver, a redhead, who went by the call sign Gopher, passed by and added, "You mean *I'll* get you out safe and sound." He smirked, but kept on his way to prepare the boat for combat.

"Those guys are the best drivers in the navy," the other SEAL, McNamara, said. He looked at Gutierrez. "No offense."

Gutierrez shrugged. He didn't take it personally.

McNamara was just as broad shouldered as Adams, about an inch taller, and Felix could make out the top of a tattoo peeking from his collar. It looked like the tip of a trident, the one carried by Poseidon, ancient Greek god of the sea, with bright red drops of blood drawn on the points. It was a warrior's tattoo, and Felix felt like he and Gutierrez and Sly would be in good hands with these two on their boat. He could trust these guys not only with his life, but with Sly's.

"So, you know how to shoot?" McNamara asked them.

"Just basic firearms training at Great Lakes," said Gutierrez, referring to the navy's boot camp for training all new recruits, on the edge of Lake Michigan.

Felix had been hunting once when he was eleven and had fired a .22 caliber rifle his father had given him. He'd been trying to hit a deer, but he missed and was relieved he'd missed. He'd actually closed his eyes when he pulled the trigger. He couldn't imagine shooting a harmless and helpless animal, and he'd never gone hunting again after that day. That was actually the day he decided he wanted to work with animals when he grew up.

But the pirates were men. They were not harmless and they were not helpless. They had attacked first and had killed Felix's friends and colleagues and they would have killed him and Sly, too, if he had been on board when their bomb went off. He wouldn't shoot an animal, but he decided he could shoot a person, if he had to. "I know how to shoot," he said.

McNamara nodded. "We're gonna get you each a weapon. Just in case."

"Not me," said Gutierrez. The SEALs looked at him like he was an alien. Then they shrugged. Adams looked at his watch. "We'll meet you on deck at eighteen thirty. That'll give us some time to meet Sly."

When the SEALs had gone, Gutierrez raised an eyebrow at Felix. Felix mouthed a silent *what?* back at him.

"You're a Marine Mammal Systems Operator," Gutierrez reminded him. "Not a Navy SEAL."

"I know," Felix said.

"Just remember that when we're out there on the water," Gutierrez told him. "These guys don't mess around . . . the SEALs *or* the pirates. Focus on Sly, not on being some kind of action hero with a week of fire-arms training."

"I just want to do my part."

"Your part is keeping Sly safe." Gutierrez sounded just like Dr. Morris — before she'd been hurt in the attack. The reminder annoyed Felix. As if he didn't know what his job was. As if he didn't care about Sly.

"My part," Felix snapped, "is the same as Sly's: support the mission. I'll do what I need to do. And so will Sly."

Gutierrez nodded. "Just remember there's no point saving the Marine Mammal Program if Sly or his handler have to die in the process."

"No one's going to die," said Felix. "At least . . . no one on our side."

Gutierrez exhaled loudly, and they walked together back to the sea lion's area on deck without another word.

The USS *Henderson* had off-loaded the last of the wounded and was now racing toward the coast of Somalia, where the small boats would be launched and the mission into the pirate bay would begin.

It was hard to believe it had been less than a day since their first mission had started. After everything he'd seen and done since the explosion on the *Ritland*, Felix didn't feel like the same person he'd been a day before. He felt shaken and angry, but also stronger and surer of himself, as if he finally felt he had a purpose in the United States Navy and a job worthy of his ambitions. He was going to save the Marine Mammal Program. And he was going to be a warrior.

13:
HIT THE BEACH

THE small black inflatable boats bobbed soundlessly in the water off the coast of Somalia. There were six boats all together, spread out in a staggered line across the bay. Each boat held a driver, a gunner, and four SEALs or marines, except for the one boat where Felix, Gutierrez, and Sly waited with their driver and two Navy SEALs.

A few miles behind the boats, the USS *Henderson* waited in the open ocean to intercept any pirates who might try to flee on the water and to provide heavy artillery backup if things didn't go as planned.

The big guns on board the boats could level the tiny buildings along the shoreline in a matter of minutes. Of course, that would kill the hostages along with the pirates, and probably a lot of innocent Somali people who had nothing to do with the pirates. Using those guns was not really an option, but the navy liked to be prepared for anything. A helicopter was also on standby to provide air support. It would take about ten minutes to reach them if it was called on.

Ten minutes, Felix thought, *could be the difference between life and death.*

He tried to shake the thought. He'd never been on a mission like this before. He didn't know what a person was supposed to think about in the quiet before it started.

An unmanned aerial vehicle — commonly known as a drone — was somewhere in the sky far above, sending live video of their mission to the command center on the *Henderson*, and to bases and secure rooms in at least three countries. For a top secret operation, an awful lot of people already knew about it. He imagined the president himself and all his advisors huddled in the White House, watching a live feed of the six tiny boats as they prepared their assault. The hair on his neck stood up. He knew he was being watched.

"It's almost go time," Felix whispered to Sly in his crate. The sea lion stared up at him, hardly seeming to blink. Felix was anxious for the mission, for the lives of the hostages and the SEALs and marines in the boats around him. He'd been told it was the president himself who would give the order to move in, and so he was also anxious to do well for the president of the United States. But he was most anxious for Sly. He had never been in combat, either. He may have been a seal, but he wasn't a SEAL.

Together, the combat newbies waited.

"We've got eyes on the Happy Meal," McNamara said, peering through his Night Optical Device. Felix wore one, too. He saw the small skiff tied to a crudely made wooden dock that jutted from the beach. They'd given the pirates' skiff the code name "Happy Meal."

The pirates they called "Nuggets," and the hostages were "Fries." Sly was nicknamed "Big Mac."

"Six Nuggets," McNamara said. "No Fries visible."

Felix followed McNamara's line of sight. He saw a small shack just past the dock. It was built on a slope to protect it from flooding, and outside there was a picnic table. Six pirates were sitting around the table. All of them had machine guns. It was a good bet that the hostages were inside that shack.

The pirates probably thought they were safe in their port, in a bay filled with explosive undersea mines, but they hadn't counted on the Navy SEALs, US Marines, or a sea lion like Sly.

The SEALs could hear one another through their earpieces. McNamara also had a wider-range antenna to communicate with the officers on board the USS *Henderson* and in the Special Operations Command Center for the Middle East. His voice would also be transmitted to a navy base in Florida, a secure room in the Pentagon, and the Situation Room in the White

House. McNamara didn't seem at all nervous about the extra attention. He was a professional doing his job.

A lot of people had to know what the SEALs were seeing before the president would be told they were ready. Once that happened, he would give the order to the admirals, who would pick up the phone to tell the captains, who would get on the radio to tell the SEAL commanders, who would pass the order to the small boats. It was a giant game of telephone, but the message was never confused. It was a simple message and Felix held his breath waiting for it.

"Happy Meal order up," the radio crackled. "Big Mac is a go."

It was as if the president had given an order directly to the sea lion. Sly, however, only took his orders from Felix. In the eyes of his partner, Felix outranked even the president of the United States.

"Here we go," Felix whispered. He called Sly from his crate. The sea lion bounded out on all four flippers, looking up expectantly. His little ears wiggled on the sides of his head. His night vision and his hearing were astounding, and Felix imagined that Sly could hear the thump of his heartbeat in his chest.

He gave one of the mine-marking clamps to Sly, who took the end in his mouth and then, with a quick gesture from Felix, dove into the water.

Adams took up a position lying down at the front of the boat with a long rifle propped in front of him. His legs were spread wide for stability and he had his eyes fixed on the shoreline through his thermal vision goggles, which let him see figures clearly in the dark. He was a trained sniper and he was taking his position for the job he had to do.

Gopher was at the wheel. McNamara stood beside him and Gutierrez had been put in the role of Felix's assistant. Gutierrez was also the only one on board without a weapon, unless you counted the serrated knife he carried on his belt. He used the "pigstick," as they called it, for cutting rope and prying the lid off of Sly's crates of fish.

Felix felt the Beretta 9mm handgun he had in his leg holster. He liked the feel of it. If he or Sly ran into danger, he felt confident he could use it. He felt a twitch in his hand. He wasn't just confident he could use it . . . he was eager to use it.

In his mind, he had to wonder if this was a rescue mission or a revenge mission. It was not a question he could answer. He wanted it to be both.

Suddenly, Sly was back, no clamp in his mouth. McNamara looked at the laptop he had with him. "One prize," he announced.

"Prize" was the code they had for the deadly explosive undersea mines.

Sly had attached his clamp to one of them. Normally, a big orange float would show its location so that the Explosive Ordnance Disposal team could come disarm it, but this mission didn't call for that. Instead, there was a locator beacon attached to the clamp so that the pilots of each of the strike force boats would know where the mines were and could avoid them.

"Good boy," Felix whispered. He gave Sly a fish, patted his side, and put another clamp in his mouth. In a flash, Sly dove again, searching for the next mine.

After that, he located another, and another after that one. Sly was getting his fill of fish, but in twenty minutes, he'd marked seven undersea mines. A human scuba diver team would have taken hours to find the same number, if they could've found them at all in the dark water. And Sly wasn't done yet.

Felix smiled each time the "prize" was counted off by the other boats to confirm they had the signal and could navigate around it.

When Sly came back with a clamp still in his mouth, Felix knew they were done. There were no more mines out there. In total, Sly had found fourteen. Even one of them could have blown a small rubber boat to pieces and ended the mission in disaster for the marines, the SEALs, the hostages, and the United States. Instead, they were ready to raid the pirate haven.

"Happy Meal order up," the radio announced again. "Marines, SEALs, you are a go to eat some Nuggets, just save us some Fries."

That was the order the SEALs had been waiting for.

The other five boats moved in, weaving their way through the pirate bay to avoid the mines that Sly had marked. The two SEAL boats would go ashore first, led by Lieutenant Coyle himself, while the three marine boats hung back. When the hostages were clear, the marines would move in to secure the area and cover the exit. Then they'd all fall out and return to the *Henderson* together.

The navy had planned the entire attack and hostage rescue to be over in less than ten minutes.

Sly and Felix and Gutierrez waited in their boat. They weren't part of the strike team. Now that the mines had been marked, their job was done.

Sly seemed content enough to go back into his crate and wait, but the others watched the shore intently. Adams still held his sniper rifle.

Felix looked through his night vision goggles as the boats approached the beach, zigging and zagging around the sea mines. As they drew closer, the drivers shut off the engines and the SEALs paddled, coordinating their rowing to move swiftly and silently through the breaking waves.

Felix glanced to the beach and saw the pirates around the picnic table laughing and joking, with no idea of the danger stalking them from the sea. One of them, however, glanced over at the ocean. He cocked his head slightly to the side and hushed the men around him. Then he stood, picking up his rifle, staring at the water, trying to make out the strange shapes moving across the surface toward the shore.

By the time he discerned the outline of the SEALs, it was too late for him.

"Send it" crackled through the radio. Felix recognized Lieutenant Coyle's voice giving the order.

At that instant, Adams squeezed his trigger. Snipers in each of the moving boats took their shots as well. All six weapons were silent, the muzzle flashes the only evidence that they had fired at all. All six pirates fell onto the sand.

By the time Felix had glanced from the boats to the beach and back to the boats again, four SEALs from each of the first two boats were gone, only a sniper and a driver still on board. The other three boats, full of the marines from the Recapture Tactics Team, were holding in the water offshore, waiting for Phase Two to begin.

"Where'd the others — ?" Felix began, but then he saw the SEALs who had been on the boats emerge from the water in scuba gear. He saw Lieutenant Coyle in the lead. They'd jumped off, swum beneath the surface, and reached the beach in under a minute. In another thirty seconds, their scuba gear was off and they crossed the sand, weapons raised. They surrounded the shack in silence.

With just hand gestures, Lieutenant Coyle told them the positions to take. It was the same way Felix talked to Sly.

When the SEAL commander clenched his fist, the first guy on the team popped the lock off the door, the second guy moved in, and three others followed.

The second squad had surrounded the shack, covering the beach from all directions. The two teams moved like the entire operation was a well-rehearsed dance, each movement connected to all the others. The only thing missing, Felix thought, was an orchestra playing for them.

Of course, the SEAL performance was deadlier than any dance.

Felix switched his goggles to a new setting: infrared vision. Through the thin walls of the shack, he could see the outlines of the SEALs approaching half a dozen others — some combination of pirates and hostages. They were bright orange figures, like shadows in reverse, with the orange fading to lighter colors at the end of their limbs, where the body temperature was lower.

Based on the movements Felix could see, the pirates were taken by surprise. There was a brief struggle, during which Felix realized he was holding his breath, dreading the sound of gunfire that never came. Within a single minute, three SEALs marched from the shack, each hauling a subdued pirate outside in plastic cuffs and dark black hoods.

The final SEAL to emerge had his arms around two men. Felix saw that it was the captain and the first mate of the *Duchess*. Both men stumbled, but the SEAL carried them forward. The squad medic gave the hostages a rapid medical check without even slowing their movement toward the boats. They'd get a more extensive medical exam when they reached the infirmary on the *Henderson*. For now, they had to get off the beach before any of Surfer Boy's other men noticed what had happened.

As the rescued hostages were loaded into one SEAL boat and the three pirate prisoners into another, Felix noticed that a fourth pirate had been left behind in the shack. That one's heat signature was starting to fade. Felix knew what that meant.

As the two SEAL boats began to paddle back into the bay, the marines moved in, driving their boats onto the beach with engines running until the last possible moment. No paddling for them. They didn't need the quiet. They needed speed and ferocity in their assault. The SEALs were silent and deadly as lightning. The marines were the earth-shaking thunder that followed.

They jumped from the boats before the hulls had even stopped sliding across the sand. The heavy M240 guns on board each of the RHIBs pointed toward the row of shacks at the top of the beach, while the marines fanned out.

At that same instant, they heard a high-pitched shout. It cracked like a whip and carried over the water, loud and sharp.

Felix gasped. The shout had come from a boy, no older than ten, standing at the top of the beach with a goat by his side. As if echoing the boy, the goat let out a long *baaahhh*.

Somehow, in the fraction of a second between the boy's shout, the goat's bleat, and the marines locking their weapons on him, they'd noticed his age, noticed he was unarmed, and held their fire. A ten-year-old boy was not a target.

The boy froze where he stood. He put his hands up.

Unfortunately, the boy's single, startled yelp had been enough of an alarm.

With a clatter of guns and angry shouts, thirty armed pirates appeared at the top of the dune. Half of them had machine guns of various sizes. A few wore bandoliers of bullets across their chests; others held clubs and machetes, antique-looking revolvers and rifles. More than one had a shoulder-fired rocket launcher, loaded and ready to fire.

At the center of the throng stood a muscular man in silk pajama pants and an open camouflage shirt, holding an Uzi submachine gun. He stood out from the rest of the pirates for one reason: even without thermal scopes or night vision goggles, his hair glowed bright blond against the night sky. Felix recognized him from the briefing.

They'd found Surfer Boy.

14:
RULES OF ENGAGEMENT

THERE was a long moment of silence as the pirates looked at the marines on the beach and at the rubber boats in the dark bay. They saw the shack where the hostages had been, the picnic table where their fellow pirates lay dead in the sand. The marines had their weapons raised.

The boat rescuing the hostages kept moving, weaving between the mines at full speed. The safe return of the hostages to the USS *Henderson* was a first priority, and the SWCC driver wouldn't stop for anything.

The boat with the three pirate prisoners, however, turned 180 degrees at full speed. The turn threw up a

148

huge wall of water, but the boat was now facing the beach and the SEALs on board had their weapons raised.

On their own boat, McNamara popped up to man one of the M240 machine guns mounted on board and aimed it a hundred yards across the water. Adams took up the mounted minigun, a machine gun capable of firing over two thousand rounds a minute. The boat bobbed on the waves, but the SEALs kept their barrels steady, pointing at the pirates on the berm at the top of the beach.

Gopher revved the engine, moved them closer to the shore.

"We don't have orders to move in," Gutierrez said.

The driver ignored him. The SEALs didn't look up from their weapons. Gutierrez looked nervously at Felix, and Felix wondered if his teammate's heart was racing as fast as his own.

In his crate, Sly was snoozing, with no idea that a gun battle between the best of the best of the United States military and a large group of heavily armed pirates was about to begin. The SEALs and marines were better trained and had better weapons, but the pirates had the high ground. The rocket launchers were a serious threat to the rubber boats in the water. If Felix were commanding this mission, he would take those guys out first. But what did he know? He was just a sea lion handler with a pistol strapped to his leg. He was in way over his head.

"Drop your weapons!" a marine officer on the beach ordered. "Hands up!"

The pirates didn't move. It was their beach in their territory. One of them shouted something at the marines in his own language, which was probably the same thing the marine had just shouted. Then the blond-haired warlord said to them in English: "Nobody has to die here. Drop your weapons and you can go, no problem."

Nobody moved. The guns stayed pointed at one another and silence settled on the beach again.

"Thirty-piece meal, Nuggets, one Special Sauce," McNamara whispered into his shoulder radio, using their code name for Surfer Boy. He glanced at the boat with the rescued hostages, now clear of the bay and racing across the open water on its way back to the *Henderson*. "Fries are away."

Felix noticed his fists were clenched so hard that he was digging his fingernails into his palms. He was hoping for artillery from the USS *Henderson* to rain down or for Adams to open up with the minigun, spraying Surfer Boy and his pals with hot lead. The marines on the beach had their M16s and the M240s mounted on their RHIBs pointed up at the pirates, too.

But then Felix saw the boy with the goat again. He had not retreated when the guns came out. He still stood among the throng of pirates.

Time slowed down.

Felix glanced over at Sly, asleep in his crate, without a care for all these man-made troubles. By instinct, the animal understood danger and risk and reward. It was what kept sea lions alive in the wild, and it was what made Sly effective at his job. But the sea lion didn't understand vengeance and would never seek it. Vengeance was a human invention.

Then again, so was justice. And the bomb attack Surfer Boy had ordered on the navy ship demanded he be brought to justice.

So was shooting all these men on the beach vengeance or justice? Was there a difference?

When Felix used to imagine pirates, he pictured the pirates from that Disney movie, with peg legs and big hats, swords and buried treasure. He did not picture this ragtag group of skinny men with mismatched weaponry, keeping children in their ranks, and holding hostages for ransom on remote beaches.

These pirates looked shabby and angry and frightened. Some of them may have helped Surfer Boy plan the bombing attack on the *Ritland*, but maybe not. Maybe the terrorists who'd done that had been the men by the picnic table and the men now held prisoner in the other Navy SEAL boat. Maybe the rest of these men were just desperate fishermen who'd turned to piracy when the warlords in control of their country pushed them to do it.

There would be no way to find out who was who if they were all dead. There was no way to bring the guilty ones to justice if the navy rained fire on them from the sky and blotted them all off the face of the earth.

There was no way to give that little boy a different life, if his life ended on this beach today.

Felix's fists unclenched. Suddenly, he didn't want vengeance. He wanted a way out, not just for himself, but for everyone on that beach, the marines, the pirates, the boy with the goat. He knew he was helpless to stop this situation. Only the men pointing the guns at one another could do that. He felt for the pistol strapped to his leg and realized he didn't want it anymore. Gutierrez was right. Felix was not a "trigger puller." He was a Marine Mammal Systems Operator, and like Dr. Morris had said, it was his job to protect and support Sly.

"Drop your weapons!" one of the marines on the beach shouted again.

"You drop your weapons!" Surfer Boy shouted back.

"We've got a phone," Adams whispered into his radio, and Felix saw a pirate on the end of the beach, holding a cell phone to his ear, talking into it.

"Drop that phone now!" a marine sergeant on the beach yelled, but the man kept talking into his phone.

"Target acquired," one SEAL sniper's voice crackled in Felix's earpiece.

The response came back from Lieutenant Coyle: "Send it."

The shot didn't make a sound, but the pirate talking on the cell phone jolted backward and fell behind the sand dune.

The men around him looked confused. One bent down to help him up, not realizing that a sniper had just shot him from across the bay. None of the other pirates seemed to have noticed, either. They must have thought the guy had tripped.

They would realize in a second or two what had happened. These men didn't have to have heard the shot to recognize the man's wound. One thing these men knew well was a gunshot wound.

One of them shouted something and the others shouted back. An argument seemed to break out among them.

As the pirates argued, the marines on the beach took small steps backward. They were spreading farther out and moving away from the target area. With each passing second, it seemed to Felix like they might avoid a bloodbath after all. If they didn't start shooting right away, maybe they wouldn't start shooting at all.

"Hey!" Surfer Boy yelled down at them. "You stop! No moving!"

The marines kept moving back slowly. They were gambling that Surfer Boy didn't want a gunfight to break out, either. Pirates were in it for the money. A gun battle with the United States Navy wouldn't be good for business.

Felix let out a breath he hadn't realized he'd been holding.

Just then, everyone heard the growl of engines. Three pickup trucks came racing down the beach. Each one was filled with armed men in camouflage. The men all had AK-47 rifles and one of the trucks had a heavy machine gun mounted on top.

"More customers," McNamara said into his radio. "Three drive-thrus; six Nuggets each. Inbound and hot."

As the trucks sped in, kicking up clouds of dust and sand, the crowd of pirates started moving forward down the beach, pushing the marines back toward the surf.

"Permission to engage drive-thrus?" McNamara asked.

No one had shot directly at any Americans yet. Was this "maintaining mission secrecy"? Could this be called self-defense? If they waited any longer, the American strike force on the beach would be surrounded and outnumbered. It felt like an eternity while they waited for the reply.

Then the answer came back from Lieutenant Coyle over the radio: "Permission granted. Light 'em up."

In that second, Adams opened fire with the minigun; McNamara fired the M240; the marines on the beach started shooting and the zip, pop, and roar of the guns tore the night sky apart.

From his crate, startled by the noise, Sly began to let out a series of high-pitched barks. The battle had begun and Felix had put his sea lion right into the middle of it.

15:
SAND AND FIRE

THE miniguns unleashed thousands of rounds of ammunition, slicing across the water in bright orange streaks. The sand burst like fireworks into the air. The pickup trucks' windows and windshields shattered, the tires burst, and the engines exploded into flames. In seconds, the trucks looked more like Swiss cheese than steel and aluminum. The gunmen who didn't dive from the vehicles in time fared no better than their trucks.

The pirates higher up on the beach above opened fire toward the boats, orange streaks of tracer fire drawing lines across the water, but their guns didn't have the range and their bullets hit nothing more than waves. The marines on shore opened fire with their M16s.

"Contact! Contact! Contact!" McNamara said into the radio to tell mission command that they had troops in contact with the enemy, a firefight in full swing. Certainly, the commanders all over the world and the president in the Situation Room in the White House could see an aerial view of the battle from the drone flying above. If the marines needed air support, they could scramble the helicopters in a heartbeat, but the navy would hesitate to risk any of their assets if they didn't have to — and those rocket launchers were a huge risk to aircraft. A squadron of marines trained in close quarters battle and a squad of SEAL Team Six operators should be able to take out a ragtag assemblage of pirates without assistance from a gunship. This was, after all, what they trained for.

Felix kept his head down and his eyes on the beach.

"Smoke!" one of the marines shouted, and they tossed smoke grenades toward the pirates. The marines all wore their thermal vision goggles, which would allow them to see human figures perfectly through the dark and the smoke.

The pirates, with no night vision goggles of any kind, were immediately blinded to the marines on the beach. They fired wildly and the Americans scrambled for safe cover.

The M240 guns thumped loudly and every shot from them hit like a sledgehammer. Any pirate unfortunate enough to find himself on the wrong end of that gun was sent whirling to the ground, never to get up again. Through his own goggles, Felix saw the goat lying on its side on the beach. He was relieved not to see the little boy. He hoped the boy had run.

Sly barked and Felix crouched down to comfort him. His duty was with his partner.

Surfer Boy took cover with three of his men behind a small broken wall. The marine sergeant on the ground directed the M240 gunners to take aim at the wall, to turn it to dust with a hail of hot lead.

Surfer Boy had other plans. With a flash and a whooshing sound from behind the wall, one of the pirates fired a rocket-propelled grenade straight at one of the marine boats on the beach.

"Incoming!" a marine shouted. They scrambled away from the boat and its big guns as the grenade rolled to a stop. A pirate made a mad dash forward, shooting his rifle. Bullets popped into the sand behind him, but he zigzagged forward, hitting one marine in the leg as he fired.

Adams, calm as could be, let go of his big gun, raised his own rifle, and snapped off two silent shots. Even with the roll of the ocean against the boat, he found his target, and the pirate fell.

Surfer Boy's grenade exploded with a blast of sand and smoke and flame. The marines dropped to the sand, covering their heads, and in that same moment, Surfer Boy directed the shoulder-fired-missile operator at his side to aim for the boats in the bay.

Felix watched for a moment in total stillness, almost like slow motion, as the missile came whistling across the water, straight at him.

"Left! Left! Left!" Adams shouted, and Gopher

spun the boat left, gunning the engines out of the path of the missile.

"Down!" McNamara yelled. The missile zipped past them, missing by less than a foot, and hit the water with a splash.

They all hit the deck. Felix dove forward and covered the opening to Sly's crate with his body. If shrapnel from the blast tore through him, at least he would be doing his duty to keep Sly safe. He shut his eyes tight.

Jets of water erupted around them and the boat rocked in the ocean, but the missile hadn't hit them. They were okay. They could stand up and return fire. They could provide cover for the marines to fall back to their remaining two boats and get away. Then they'd call in air support and take out Surfer Boy and his men from the sky. It was all possible and would all be okay, Felix thought.

He opened his eyes and stood.

That was when the second explosion came. The missile had set off an undersea mine.

The boat heaved beneath Felix, launching him upward like a springboard. An invisible fist punched him in the back, the force of the blast hurling him forward. He felt himself twisting around in the air and saw the ocean surface below him, racing up. The boat flipped, torn open. The last thing he saw before plunging under the dark waves with the wind knocked out of him was the side of Sly's crate, blasted open.

He didn't see Sly.

16:
BEACHED BLOND

FELIX'S ears rang. As he broke the surface of the water, gasping for air, he choked and spat salt water. He'd lost his night vision goggles, so all he could make out through the dark and the smoke were the bright orange streaks of gunfire and the tongues of flame from the beach.

He'd been thrown far from his own boat, he couldn't see any of the other crew, and he couldn't hear a single thing.

He tread water, unsure what to do.

What if Sly was injured? What if he was bleeding and floating away, helpless in an unfamiliar ocean? A wounded sea lion in the open water would be shark food in minutes.

So, in fact, would a wounded person.

The boat with the SEALs and the prisoners still on it had moved closer to the beach. They unleashed all their firepower on the small wall from which the rocket had been fired.

The marines had fallen back to their boats and, as the first one pulled out through the breaking waves and into the bay, the others kept shooting. Once that boat was clear of the beach, it turned and opened fire to cover the next boat's exit. It was a coordinated withdrawal, not a retreat. Even as the marines left, they never stopped fighting.

The boats weaved their way across the bay toward the sinking RHIB. Felix saw one of the marines reach over and scoop a limp figure from the water. He couldn't tell who it was in the dark, Gopher, Adams, McNamara, or Gutierrez. He could, however, tell that the figure wasn't moving. By the light of the burning boat, he saw another figure swimming through the water, with one arm, pulling another person along.

When the marines reached them, they helped the injured man on board and then the swimmer was able to hoist himself up. Felix saw it was Gutierrez and that the injured man was Adams. Felix was relieved his friend was safe. Lastly, he saw Gopher pulled into the remaining SEAL boat. Now Felix knew that the driver was safe, Gutierrez was safe, one SEAL was injured, one SEAL was unconscious . . . and one sea lion was missing.

As his hearing returned, Felix could make out the sound of helicopter blades beating against the air. That explained the marines falling back off the beach. The air assault was coming in.

Felix tried to whistle, to call Sly to him. He didn't see the animal's head poking from the water anywhere. He listened for his partner's high-pitched bark, but his ears still rang, and with the noise of the machine guns firing back at the beach and the boat engines buzzing and now the helicopter coming in, it was hopeless. Poor Sly, with his super-sensitive hearing, must have been in agony.

The marine boat got to Felix, and Gutierrez himself leaned over the side and grabbed his arm. Felix gave a strong kick in the water as Gutierrez lifted, and he climbed on board.

"Sly?" Gutierrez asked.

Felix shook his head. "I don't know." He looked at Adams, whose face was bloody, one eye swollen shut. He had one arm hanging limp at his side, but, strangely to Felix, still had his rifle slung across his chest. McNamara was propped against the hull, eyes closed, but breathing. Adams used his good hand to press a bandage to the bloody wound on the side of McNamara's head.

"He gonna be okay?" Felix asked.

"It takes more than a sea mine to kill a SEAL," Adams said. "He'll wake up with a headache."

"You okay?" Felix asked.

Adams shrugged. "Just another beautiful day in the United States Navy."

"Did you see what happened to Sly?"

Adams shook his head.

Just then, an Apache helicopter zipped overhead, straight for the beach. Its missiles zipped for the walls and dunes where pirates had taken cover. The mounted guns on the Apache's nose raked up and down the beach. The missiles hit the shacks and dunes with white-hot explosions and the night sky glowed red. The remaining pirates didn't stand a chance. Those who could run, ran.

And like that, the battle was over. The Apache peeled off to return to the ship.

"Thanks for the assist, Hawkeye One," Lieutenant Coyle said over the radio. "Sorry to get you out of bed in the middle of the night. I know you boys like to sleep in."

"Roger that," the Apache pilot responded. "Next time make some coffee."

"Aye aye," said Lieutenant Coyle.

The boats were all overfull now, since one had been lost in the assault, and they were on their way out of the bay.

"We can't leave yet," Felix said.

"Orders are to beat it out of here," the SWCC driver on this boat said. "Everyone's accounted for."

"Sly's still out there!" Felix objected.

The squad leader, a marine corps sergeant, spoke up. "The sea lion?"

"He's a member of the team," said Felix.

"I can't go back for a sea lion," the sergeant said. "I've got casualties. They need to get to the medics."

Felix didn't know what to say. He didn't want to risk human lives by delaying their return, but his job was to protect Sly and Sly was still out there.

"Sergeant!" Adams called from his spot by McNamara. "We have a member of the team unaccounted for. We go back."

"I'm not authorized to —"

"We. Go. Back." Adams didn't move a muscle, but his tone of voice left no room for argument, not even from a person as tough as a marine corps sergeant.

The sergeant nodded and grabbed his radio. "This is Bravo Two Actual," he said into his radio. "We're going back in. Big Mac is missing."

"Roger that," Lieutenant Coyle responded without hesitation. "Alpha One Actual on your six."

With that, the driver turned their boat around and the SEAL boat fell in directly behind them to provide cover. The other boats turned and held their position, watching the beach from a distance to provide cover if the remaining pirates were stupid enough to come back for another fight. It didn't seem likely that they would. The fires of the battle still burned on the sand.

The boats had to slow their engines as they weaved their way forward. Thirteen mines remained below the surface.

Felix borrowed a set of thermal vision goggles and scanned the water's surface. He saw no sign of Sly. He scanned the beach. The smoke and the fire were bright outlines against the black and gray shells of the shacks and the ruined trucks. He forced himself to look at the bodies littering the dunes. They were all human and none were moving. He didn't let his gaze linger. He kept scanning, side to side.

Suddenly, he saw movement from the edge of his vision. A person sat up. The figure rose from the ground and rolled another body off itself. A pirate had hidden from the gunfire beneath the body of another pirate. The man stood up and Felix immediately recognized him, even in the ghostly outline of the thermal image through the goggles. It was Surfer Boy, the man responsible for all this death, all this violence. He was moving along the beach now, staying crouched low, glancing out at the dark bay.

"I got him," Adams said. Felix glanced down and saw that Adams had let go of McNamara's bandage and was now in a sniper's position, with the gun resting on the hull of the boat and his good arm holding it up, finger on the trigger.

"If you've got a shot, take it," Lieutenant Coyle said over the radio. Everyone with goggles had seen Surfer Boy. They were still determined to accomplish their mission, to capture this warlord dead or alive.

Adams squeezed the trigger. The muzzle flashed in the dark and the sand just to the left of Surfer Boy's bright blond head kicked up with the impact of a bullet. Surfer Boy ducked for cover behind a heap of wood and tin that had once been someone's beachfront shack. Adams had missed.

Felix looked away from the rubble. Let the SEALs worry about Surfer Boy. He had to keep searching for Sly. He tuned out everything else, searched the beach and the water for the sea lion, and then he saw something with heart-sinking clarity: Sly's hulking shape on the beach just above where the waves were breaking. They rolled up over him, with foam and spray, and Sly didn't move.

The sea lion had beached himself, probably in fright at the huge noise of the sea mine explosion.

Felix wondered exactly when Sly had gotten to the beach. If he had been there when the Apache helicopter opened fire, there was no way he could have survived. Was he injured? Was he bleeding? Was he already dead?

There was only one way to find out and only one thing for Felix to do.

"I found Sly," he said. "Take me in."

"Surfer Boy is still a threat," Adams said, without looking up from his rifle scope. "He's armed."

"So am I," said Felix, touching the Beretta 9mm still strapped to his leg. "And I've got you to cover me."

"Let's do this," the marine sergeant said. "Back to the beach."

The marines on board readied their weapons. They might not have liked the idea of risking their lives again for a sea lion, but they were professionals and they were ready.

"We're going in for Big Mac," Adams said into the radio.

"Roger that," Lieutenant Coyle replied. "We've got you covered."

"Hang in there, Sly," Felix whispered to himself as their boat rode the swelling waves to the fiery beach. "I'm coming for you, pal."

17:
BIRD-DOGGING

THEY hit the beach hard. They were marines, not SEALs, and they landed like a wrecking ball, a dozen boots crashing into the wet sand, M16s up, and fingers on their triggers. Spent shell casings crunched beneath their feet. For Felix, participating in a combat beach landing was much different from watching from a distance. There was a rush, a thrill alongside the fear, and Felix's mind felt sharp and focused. Like when he was underwater in the hull of the *Ritland*, he felt his fear and he didn't let it stop him.

He jumped out of the small boat, leaving Gutierrez and Adams on board with McNamara and the SWCC driver. Two marines stayed on either side, kneeling in the sand, and Adams took up the big, mounted M240 to provide heavy firepower if it was needed. The SEAL sniper on Lieutenant Coyle's boat, floating out past the breaking waves, kept his sights locked on the rubble where Surfer Boy was hiding.

"Let's move," the marine sergeant barked, and he, along with four more marines, escorted Felix fifty feet across the beach toward the wet sand where Sly lay. As they moved forward, Felix unholstered his pistol and pulled it out, feeling the weight of it in both hands. He thumbed off the safety, just in case he had to use it.

Everything on the beach but the marines was still . . . even Sly.

When they reached the big sea lion, stretched out across the sand like a bather in the moonlight, the marines formed a secure perimeter, and Felix knelt beside the animal. He shoved the pistol back into his holster and put his hands on Sly's side.

"Hey, buddy, it's me, I'm here," he whispered. For one terrible moment, he felt nothing, but then, there was the unmistakable rise and fall of a giant furry chest taking a breath. Sly lifted his head, his neck bending back toward Felix, looking at him sideways.

Felix broke into a smile and Sly broke the quiet with a bark. "Aoof! Aoof! Aoof!"

"Let me check you out, good boy," Felix said. He ran his hands up and down Sly's body, searching for wounds. He felt none. The sea lion had just run scared and played dead. He'd survived the explosion and the helicopter assault without a scratch on him. Felix gave him the signal to get up and Sly obeyed, hopping up onto his flippers.

"Very good!" he said cheerily, in the voice he used to praise his partner. The tone of voice sounded so out of place on this beach in the aftermath of the battle. Felix noticed one of the marines glance at another one and smirk.

He felt bad he didn't have any fish to reward Sly with, but his partner seemed happy enough not to be alone anymore. Felix didn't care if the marines thought he was weird; he bent down and gave his partner a hug. Sly leaned onto his back flippers and tail, bringing his body up tall, and he wrapped his front flippers around Felix for a wet, stinky, sea lion embrace.

"We good to go, sailor?" the sergeant asked him without looking. He still had his M16 aimed at the rubble where Surfer Boy was hiding.

"Good to go, Sergeant," Felix replied. "Big Mac is ready."

"Let's roll out," the sergeant said.

They moved back to the boat, the line of marines keeping Sly and Felix surrounded for security. Felix walked backward, beckoning Sly to stay with him. The sea lion took a hopping flipper-step for every backward step Felix took and like that, with their own team of bodyguards, they made it all the way back to the boat.

Felix climbed on, then Sly jumped aboard and gave a greeting bark to Gutierrez.

"Nice to see you too, pal," Gutierrez said. Sly rocked his head from side to side playfully.

The marines worked together to push the boat out backward through the breaking waves, while Adams kept the gun aimed for the beach to shoot at anything that moved while their backs were turned.

Less than ten minutes after they'd landed, they were off the beach again, motoring their way out of the bay with hours to spare before sunrise. There was one marine who'd taken a gunshot to the leg, and Adams and McNamara had sustained injuries in the mine explosion, but they'd rescued the hostages and none of the American strike force had been killed. Even though Surfer Boy was still at large, the pirates had fared much, much worse. His private army of criminals and terrorists was decimated. Felix only wished they'd been able to arrest the man himself.

Adams had returned to his position with the rifle and aimed back at the pile of rubble, hoping Surfer Boy would stick his blond head out enough to take him down.

"No shot," he said into the radio. He sighed and lifted his head from the rifle, leaning back and looking at his wounded friend. McNamara was awake again, bloodied, but alive.

"Bad day for hunting, I guess," McNamara said.

"If we were hunting, we could flush him out with a bird dog," Adams said.

Suddenly, McNamara's eyes brightened. Adams's, too. They turned to look at Felix and at Sly. Adams cocked his head slightly to the side.

"No way," said Felix. "I just got Sly to safety."

"He'll be safe," said Adams. "We'll cover him just like we covered you."

Felix looked at Gutierrez, who shook his head and mouthed the word *no*.

He looked at the marines and the SEALs on the boat, who would do whatever was asked of them, no matter the risk, to accomplish their mission. Then he looked at Sly, who would also do whatever was asked of him, not for the mission, but for his handler . . . for Felix.

"If we let Surfer Boy get away, he'll attack more ships, hurt more people," Adams said. "And some other group of guys is going to have to come after him, risking their lives. We can end this today. Sly can help us end this."

Felix took a deep breath. He looked at Gutierrez. "We have to," he said.

"That's not what Sly's for," said Gutierrez. "It's not right."

"I know it's not right," said Felix. "But it's war. What's right about any of it?"

He nodded to Adams, who got on the radio and told Lieutenant Coyle to hold. They were going to take one last crack at Surfer Boy.

"I'm not sending any guys on shore again," Lieutenant Coyle responded. "Phase Two is over."

"Roger that, L-T," Adams said, smirking at Felix. "We're just doing a little bird-dogging."

"I don't even want to know what that means," the lieutenant responded.

18:
A KIND OF JUSTICE

SLY was trained to hunt for a variety of undersea mines and could even tell the difference between mines made by different countries. Sly was also trained to identify and pursue swimmers. Sly was absolutely not trained to identify pirates, go onto a beach, and run them down. He might not even understand what Felix was asking him to do.

Felix wasn't even sure *he* understood. And he wasn't sure he was comfortable with it, either, but Adams was right. If they didn't take out Surfer Boy now, more people would suffer. More people would die. He thought once more about the little boy with the goat. That boy had just been witness to a bloody battle brought on because Surfer Boy organized the hijacking of a cargo ship and the bombing of a navy destroyer. How many more boys would have to witness such things, how many more boys would be put in danger if Surfer Boy escaped?

Felix knew that every animal rights organization in the world would be enraged if they knew what he was about to ask Sly to do. And they would be right to be upset. This wasn't fair and it wasn't safe.

"This is not what the Navy Marine Mammal Program is for," Gutierrez said. "This is just not right."

"I know," said Felix. "Nothing about war is right. But sometimes you have to do the wrong thing in order to make things right."

With that, he turned away from Gutierrez, and made a hand signal for Sly to be alert for instruction, the first step in the process. Then he gave him the command to hunt for a swimmer. Sly tossed his head back, wet fur gleaming, and threw the weight of his body sideways over the hull, flinging himself into the dark ocean. The boat rocked as the animal leaped from it, and settled again on the water when he disappeared.

Adams fixed the sight of his rifle back on the heap of rubble that hid Surfer Boy.

Everyone waited.

The trained sea lion knew to pursue his target, even if that target fled to land. What Felix didn't know was if Sly would go onto land looking for his target if he didn't find him in the water at all. This would be a test for Sly like no other, and if he did get on land, there was no guarantee that Surfer Boy or another pirate wouldn't open fire on him the moment he popped from the water. Because Surfer Boy had seen the marines come to Sly's rescue, he would know that the sea lion was in the navy, and that would make him a target.

Minutes passed, when suddenly, Sly's narrow head broke the surface beside the boat again. He hadn't found anything. Felix glanced at the beach. Lieutenant Coyle's voice rattled in his ear: "No movement."

Felix signaled Sly to go down and look once more. He pointed at the beach and Sly dove. Minutes later, he saw the outline of the sea lion's gleaming body in the breaking waves, riding the surf into shore. Sly slid onto the sand and immediately popped onto his flippers. His head swept side to side while his snout and whiskers worked the air. Even his little ears seemed to be searching. And then he started to move, bounding forward in a motion that made him look like an inchworm crossed with a German shepherd. All six hundred pounds of him bobbed across the dark beach, straight for the rubble heap where Surfer Boy was hiding.

"Come on out," Adams whispered. "Show your dumb blond head."

Surfer Boy didn't show his head, didn't show so much as a single blond hair. He knew snipers were out there. Felix wanted to whistle to call Sly back, but the sea lion vanished over the dunes and charged behind the rubble heap, where the SEALs couldn't see him. They couldn't protect him, either.

And then, the night silence was broken by a scream. It was not a goatherd boy's scream this time, but a full grown man's, and it was followed by the *rat tat tat* of an Uzi submachine gun.

"Sly!" Felix shouted.

"Shh!" Adams snapped at him.

The blond-haired pirate dashed from his hiding spot, running low and zigzagging, firing his weapon wildly. The muzzle of the Uzi flashed bright in the night, rounds zipping out every which way. The bright streaks popped into the sky and slashed across the surface of the water, pinging up little spouts and digging brief bullet holes in the ocean.

Surfer Boy wasn't aiming and his weapon didn't even have the range to hit the inflated boats in the bay, but the chaos was enough to keep the snipers from hitting him.

He ran so fast that for an instant, it looked like he would get away.

We failed, Felix thought. *And because of me, Sly was shot. It's my fault. I should never have —*

Suddenly, Sly burst out from behind the rubble heap. Surfer Boy glanced back and saw the sea lion coming after him, all fangs and fur, and he stumbled, tripping. Sly caught up to him, his jaws opening, as if he were going to place a clamp on the man's ankle . . . except he had no clamp. Sly bit down and held Surfer Boy in the vise grip of his jaws, his teeth digging into the flesh.

Surfer Boy screamed again, but this time he wasn't able to fire off his weapon. He dropped it as Sly dragged him across the beach toward the water. The blond man clawed at the sand, tried to kick and squirm free, but Sly was much too strong. He pulled Surfer Boy about thirty feet before letting go, giving a triumphant bark to let Felix know he'd found the target, and he continued moving for the waterline on his own. He wasn't trained to drag a person back to the boat.

Free from the jaws of the big mammal, Surfer Boy scrambled back to his feet and dove to recover his Uzi.

Lieutenant Coyle's voice crackled once more through all their earpieces: "Send it."

Adams took the shot and Surfer Boy never reached his weapon. He fell face-first onto the beach and a dark spot formed on the back of his blond head. Through the view of the goggles, it looked like a shadow growing over his skull. Adams fired a second shot, a standard Navy SEAL double tap.

"Special Sauce is down," Adams said into the radio.

Lieutenant Coyle radioed back to the command center on the ship, which relayed the message up the chain of command. The mission was over and the man responsible for the pirate attacks in the Gulf of Aden and the bombing of the USS *Ritland* "was down." It would have been better to have captured him and put him on trial for his crimes, but he'd given them no choice. One way or another, justice had been done.

Felix knew that he and Sly had played an important role, but he also knew that the mission was top secret. He could never tell the amazing things his sea lion had done, but he would know and Sly would know, and that was a bond they would always have.

Except Sly wasn't back at the boat yet.

When Felix looked for him through the goggles, he saw his big dark shape just below the surface, with only his head poking out from the water. He was swimming for their boat slowly, only one flipper pushing forward. The other left a trail of blood streaming out behind him in the water.

All the pride left Felix like the air leaving a deflating balloon. Sly had been shot.

The ocean current pushed against Sly and even though his one flipper was still powerful, it wasn't powerful enough. He was turning to the side, drifting, and being pushed in a circle back toward shore.

Felix didn't ask for permission and he didn't hesitate. He jumped overboard into the water and swam as hard and as fast as he ever had in his life to reach his injured partner before he lost him forever.

19:
A LION'S PRIDE

SLY'S head and neck pushed against the current, looking sideways at Felix in the water. His eyes were glassy, as always, but there was something off about them, a lazy distance to his gaze like he was looking at Felix but not really seeing him, like a person just woken from a nap, still half dreaming.

"It's me, pal," Felix said in as comforting a tone as he could manage. Sly couldn't understand the words, but at least he'd recognize the voice and feel its reassurance. "You did great. You're gonna be okay."

A rolling swell of the ocean pushed Felix away and filled his mouth with salt water. He spat and crawled back over to Sly, reaching out as gently as he could. He remembered all too well being bitten and he didn't want to startle the animal, especially not in the water, where even injured, Sly could be dangerous. In fact, being injured made him more dangerous. A wounded animal was an animal most likely to attack.

Sly didn't move to bite Felix, though. He just stared back at him through his distant, dark eyes and rolled on his side, presenting his neck and his belly up toward the sky. It was a signal of submission, of weakness, of surrender. Sly was telling Felix he'd given up.

Felix wasn't about to give up on Sly. He rested the sea lion's head against his chest and wrapped his arms around him, like he was giving the sea lion a hug, and then he began to swim backward using his legs, dragging Sly along through the ocean. The current was pushing them both now and it took all the strength Felix had to keep going. Sly was too heavy. They were slowing. They weren't going to make it. He kept kicking through the water, long after he had any strength left.

Suddenly, the marines in their boat were behind him, and two guys bent over the side to hang on to Felix's shoulders. He didn't let go of Sly, but now at least he didn't need to kick to keep from drifting away.

"What can we do?" the sergeant on board asked.

"We have to get him out of the water somehow," Felix said. "But we need to be gentle. He could bite if he gets too frightened. I'll try to keep him calm."

The sergeant had an idea. He tossed a nylon rope over the side, which Felix could tie around Sly and use to haul him on board. That way, there were no strange hands grabbing at him and no one but Felix for him to bite.

Once the knot was secured and checked for tightness, Felix gave the okay to start hoisting. He stayed in the water and kept his hands on Sly's side, whispering to him that it was all right, that he was safe, that no one would hurt him.

The marines grunted and strained as they hoisted the animal up. The boat tilted. The side opposite Sly rose out of the water over a foot while Sly's side almost sank completely under. Because it was so low in the water, Felix had no problem lifting himself on board, so that he was face-to-face with Sly as he slid into the hull and the boat settled once more.

"Big Mac is on board," the sergeant said into the radio.

"Affirmative. Move out," Lieutenant Coyle responded, and the boats turned and set out at full speed from the bay.

Felix knelt on the deck beside Sly and immediately began applying emergency medical care.

"I need some help here," Felix said.

Every sailor assigned to the Marine Mammal Program learned the basics of veterinary care for the animals they looked after, so Felix had some idea of what to do. He'd asked enough questions of Dr. Morris over the years that he felt he could save Sly.

The marines of the Recapture Tactics Team had also all received combat first aid training, and even better, they had a navy corpsman on board, an experienced combat medic. The corpsmen were trained to handle human injuries, but humans and sea lions were both mammals, so the basics of emergency care were roughly the same. First step, they had to stop the bleeding.

Felix found the wounds in his partner's front flipper. Surfer Boy's Uzi had fired so rapidly that he'd hit Sly four times in his wild rampage. There was a nearly straight line of bullet holes from the top of Sly's flipper, where it met his chest, to the end of the flipper, which he used to support himself when walking on land. Blood seeped from all four wounds.

"We need to apply pressure," Felix instructed, pointing at the three bullet holes farthest from Sly's body. One of the marines grabbed some bandages from the corpsman's bag and started to pack the wounds and wrap them tightly. "I'll need your help with this one," Felix told the corpsman. "The bullet's still in there. We need to get it out."

"I've never done battlefield surgery on a sea lion before," the corpsman said.

"Well, the sea lion's never been in a gunfight before, so I guess it's a day of firsts for everyone," Felix replied.

The corpsman nodded and took out a set of sterile surgical pliers. Felix pressed himself to the side of Sly's body and stroked his head. He whispered and cooed, to keep Sly calm, and then rested his arm across his partner's chest. If the sea lion bucked and jolted to get free, they couldn't really stop him. He was far too strong. But Felix hoped his own body language would keep Sly docile and keep him from moving too much. Normally, for a medical procedure like this, an animal as strong and wild as a California sea lion would be strapped down and sedated with drugs. There was no time for all of that.

When Felix nodded that he was ready, the medic dug his pliers into the open wound. Felix felt Sly's whole body tense, felt the rib cage heave and the rear flippers twitch.

"Shhh, shhh, it's okay, it's okay," Felix whispered

directly into Sly's funny little ear. Their faces were so close together that Sly could have bit Felix's nose off in a moment of panic. Gutierrez knelt and put his whole body across Sly's tail, doing his part to hold the animal down for the operation. Someone shined a dim red flashlight down on Sly's flipper.

The corpsman pulled the bloody bullet out, gripped in his pliers, and Felix packed and bound the wound. Luckily, sea lions had a far higher tolerance for pain than humans did. Sly barely flinched. He lay flat on the deck and breathed as they bounced through the waves toward their ship.

In the first moment of calm since the siege of the pirate bay began, Felix glanced around the boat. In the moonlight, he could make out the grim faces of the battle-hardened marines, dirty and blackened and bloodied from the gunfight. He could see Adams, no longer manning his weapon, but holding the injured McNamara in his arms, like they were brothers huddled in a backyard tree fort. Gutierrez was sitting up again, looking back at Felix, a mixture of relief and disappointment across his face.

Felix felt the same thing in himself. He didn't say a word, just looked down at his wounded partner, an innocent animal dragged into a senseless human conflict. It wasn't his fault the pirates and terrorists had done what they did, and it wasn't his fault the navy needed his abilities. He was caught up in it all, like that little boy on the beach. Sly's work had helped save the hostages and had taken out a murderous warlord pirate. Any human soldier would have been proud of wounds sustained in such an effort. Felix wondered what pride a sea lion could feel.

"You're gonna be okay, Sly," he told the sea lion, patting his chest gently. "I'm sorry this happened to you."

Sly lifted his head lightly at the sound of his name and let out a low, wheezing breath. Then he dropped his head again, exhausted, but alive.

When they got back to the USS *Henderson*, a helicopter was standing by to fly Sly and the more seriously injured marines and SEALs to the naval base in Bahrain. Adams helped load McNamara on board, while the marine who'd been shot in the leg hobbled on board himself. Sly was strapped into a special harness and hoisted up. An IV drip was hooked in to replace some of his fluids.

On deck, Lieutenant Coyle shouted over the roar of the helicopter into Felix's ear. "A veterinary team will meet you at the helipad in Bahrain. You think he'll make it?"

Felix nodded.

"They don't give medals of valor to sea lions," Lieutenant Coyle said. "But you and I know they should."

He shook Felix's hand and Felix boarded the chopper to fly with Sly to Bahrain. Adams sat across from him beside McNamara's stretcher. SEALs always stayed with their "swim buddy," just like Marine Mammal Systems Operators always stayed with their mammal. Or, at least, stayed as close as they could. There were deep and watery places on this earth where Felix could never follow Sly.

As the engine pitch rose and the *womp womp womping* of the rotor blades lifted the helicopter through the air, Felix unstrapped the Beretta 9mm handgun from his leg. He lifted and reached across Sly's harness to hand it back to Adams, who took it with just a nod. The battle was over, and neither Felix nor Sly needed to be warriors anymore.

20:
BATTLE CRY

"**I READ** your report on the operation in the Gulf of Aden, Petty Officer Pratt," Commander Jackson said to Felix, leaning back in her chair as the gulls of the San Diego Bay circled the water outside her window. It was a warm California afternoon, but the atmosphere inside Commander Jackson's office was decidedly cool . . . and not because of the air-conditioning. "I found it to be clear, concise, and . . ." She searched for the word.

"Unequivocal, ma'am?" Felix suggested.

"Unequivocal." Commander Jackson smiled. "Yes. You did not equivocate. You made your point uncompromisingly. I disagree with the point you made, however, and I added my own notes to that effect before passing the report up to command."

"Yes, ma'am, I understand." Felix nodded. The words were polite, but the tone was clear. He was being scolded. "May I ask to what part you objected?"

"We are a military force," she said. "And we are at war with pirates and terrorists who will stop at nothing to do us harm. You have firsthand experience of their brutality from the *Ritland* attack."

"Yes, ma'am, I do," said Felix, remembering all too well the explosion, the carnage, the death. It had only happened a week and a half ago.

"You were accurate in your description of events as they affected this recent Marine Mammal Systems deployment," she continued. "You did admirable, creative, and brave work. You made us all proud."

"Thank you, ma'am."

Commander Jackson made a face like she had sucked on something sour. "I wish you had left it there in your report. I would like to know why you felt the need to add your own opinions about the nature of the mission . . . a mission which you seemed to feel was important, I might add."

"Respectfully, I came to believe it is not right to use our mammals in dangerous operations," Felix said.

"Even if the danger they face can save human lives?"

"Even so, ma'am," Felix said. "I'm proud of what we did, but I wouldn't feel right putting another animal through what Sly went through. By using sea lions and dolphins in potential combat situations, we are turning them into targets."

"Well, Petty Officer Pratt," Commander Jackson said. "You'll get your wish. I have received word that the Marine Mammal Program will be phased out over the next few years. I assured them that nothing could replace the unique force protection abilities of our dolphins and sea lions. I might have convinced them, too, but your report gave even more strength to the arguments of the politicians who want to shut us down. They've gone into the final testing phase for the robots."

"I'm sorry, ma'am. I never intended to —"

She raised her hand to cut him off. "It's not entirely your fault," she said. "The program is over sixty years old. Technology was bound to catch up with it."

Felix nodded, but stood in silence. He had yet to be dismissed by his commanding officer. She looked at him wistfully. She no longer seemed angry at him, just disappointed that her program was going to be shut down, that Felix and Sly hadn't saved it like she thought they would. Felix surprised himself by not feeling any disappointment whatsoever. He had wanted to prove himself and to prove that his sea lion could do anything. He had done that, but it had cost him too much. It had cost Sly too much.

Commander Jackson interrupted the long silence. "Sly is healing?"

"Yes, ma'am," Felix said. "He's received excellent care and will regain full use of his pectoral flipper in a few months."

"Good," she said. "Our program will continue to operate until we get orders to pack it in, and Sly is one of the best we've got."

"Ma'am, I understand if you want me to transfer —"

"Nonsense," she cut him off again. Interruption was rude, but it was an officer's privilege. Her voice grew softer now. "You, too, are one of the best we've got, and I hope you will stay with us until the program is phased out. I can assure you, there will be no further combat deployments for you or for Sly. You'll be here in San Diego, doing the usual training, study, search and recovery. There are a lot of university students who are eager to learn all they can about sea lions' unique intelligence as long as this program still exists. You will work with them. Does that suit you?"

"Yes, ma'am." Felix smiled. She could have just ordered him, but she had respected him enough to ask.

Commander Jackson returned his smile. "I mean it when I said we're all proud of the work you did out there. You saved a lot of lives and helped bring a terrorist to justice. I know it wasn't easy and I know you feel guilty about Sly's injuries. No matter what anyone says, you did the right thing. Understood?"

"Yes, ma'am," Felix said one more time. He didn't sound all that convincing. He wasn't sure he believed it himself. He'd learned that in the fog of war and in the heat of battle, right and wrong were hard to see and harder still to do. He'd done what he felt he had to; he just wasn't sure he wanted to call it the right thing or the wrong thing.

"Dismissed," Commander Jackson told him, and he snapped her a crisp salute and left.

It wasn't a long way from her office to the veterinary facility, and he ran it so he could get there fast. The cavernous space was filled with pools and tanks and operating tables and a big crane for lifting and moving dolphins and sea lions.

He weaved his way around the room to the small pool where Sly was in the water, with a veterinary technician standing beside him to help him swim in a straight line using both his flippers.

"Afternoon, Felix," the technician called over to him.

"Afternoon," he responded. "How's my man doing today?"

"He's an excellent patient," the technician told him.

"Of course he is," said Felix. "He's Sly!"

At the sound of his name, Sly lifted his head out of the water and gave Felix a long, loud, wall-shaking bark of "Aoof! Aoof! Aoof!" and Felix did it right back to him.

"Aoof! Aoof! Aoof!" Felix laughed. They really did have their own battle cry now, forged in fire and friendship, and there was no animal on earth he would have rather shared it with.

AUTHOR'S NOTE

THIS book is a work of fiction. While the United States Navy Marine Mammal Program is real and does use thirty-five California sea lions in a variety of roles, there is no such sailor as Felix Pratt, nor such a sea lion as Sly.

I did, however, base much of what Sly is capable of doing on the very real workings of the Marine Mammal Program. Since 1960, the navy has used marine mammals like dolphins, orcas, beluga and pilot whales as well as sea lions, in a lot of different ways. They locate equipment on the sea floor, detect and mark undersea mines so that they can be disarmed, and patrol ports to prevent swimmer attacks. They are also used for research, in partnership with universities around the country, to learn more about the unique intelligence and capabilities of these remarkable creatures.

The navy claims the program is being phased out, with many of the dolphins and sea lions to be replaced by underwater robots beginning in 2017, although the program will not be entirely eliminated. The navy cites a lot of reasons for phasing out the program, some of which I explore in the story: cost of the program, potential danger to the animals, and advances in technology. There are, however, some things that these animals can do better than any human invention and for that reason, the navy continues to deploy them. As I write this, there are at least twenty dolphins and ten sea lions currently operating in the Black Sea to counter Russian military moves in the region. The navy isn't saying much about what these creatures are up to, but their deployment certainly raised tensions in the region when word got out they were there.

It is important to remember that these are wild

animals, trained as well as they may be, and there are dangers involved in working with them. As recently as April 2014, a 29-year-old civilian contractor who worked with dolphins and sea lions for the navy drowned under mysterious circumstances during training exercises.

There are also moral questions raised by using captive animals in warfare. A senior vice president of People for the Ethical Treatment of Animals (PETA), an animal rights advocacy group, framed the problem to a reporter for *MintPress News* when she said: "Why in 2014 are we relying on dolphins for anything in the military, when we have come to an understanding that marine mammals are sophisticated and intelligent?" she asked. "They don't belong to us. They are not our weapons, not our toys."

As far as the navy claims, their mammals are not used on dangerous mission like the one I sent Felix and Sly on in this story, but the animals are certainly capable of performing in combat, and there have been rumors since the program began about killer dolphins and sea lions. The navy denies these rumors.

One undeniable truth: Modern-day pirates are very real and are a very real threat to cargo ships rounding the Horn of Africa, as well as to the villages on the shores of Somalia from which they operate. Warlords and gangsters have found that they can exploit the impoverished fishermen along the coast, driving them to piracy for a cut of the profits from ransoming cargo ships and their crew.

At its height in the late 2000s, modern pirates were stealing between $900 million and $3 billion dollars a year, but thanks to efforts by the international community, including the deployment of US warships in a joint antipiracy task force like the one Felix and Sly joined, piracy incidents have dropped off in recent years. Their rate of success has greatly declined and the wealthy backers of the pirates seem to have decided that the costs of piracy are just not worth the risks.

One of the most famous failed pirate hijacking attempts is the 2009 siege of the *Maersk Alabama*, dramatized in the film *Captain Phillips*. Four pirates seized an American cargo ship, fled with the captain as their hostage, and were stopped by US Navy warships and members of SEAL Team 6, including an elite group of snipers and combat swimmers. The hostage was safely rescued and a clear message was sent to other would-be pirates: If you take hostages, you may forfeit your life. The story of the *Maersk* operation was a source of inspiration for some of the incidents in *Tides of War: Honor Bound*, but I did take a lot of liberties and make up a lot of elements.

Ultimately, the men and women of the Marine Mammal Program and of the US Navy work very hard, with a great deal of professionalism, in order to avoid violent confrontations and loss of life like I described in this story. In real life, there are far fewer explosions, but there is also far more bravery.

WHAT HAPPENS WHEN MAN'S BEST FRIEND GOES TO WAR?

Read on for a sneak peek of
Dog Tags #1: Semper Fido!

It was a mile back to the medevac site, and I couldn't carry my best friend anymore.

I stopped and felt the limp weight slung over my shoulder, too heavy to go on. I'd carried him this way a hundred times in training. Two hundred times, maybe. But this wasn't training.

This was real.

My muscles burned and my ears still rang from the explosion. I tried to listen for the distant *wump wump wump* of a helicopter coming in, but all I could hear was the rapid *thump thump thump* of my heartbeat.

Or was it Loki's heartbeat, pulsing desperately next to my ear?

My shirt was covered in blood. Only some of it was mine.

No help could reach us down in this rocky ravine, exposed to sniper fire from all sides. I had to get across the dry riverbed and over that hill.

The riverbed.

Piles of rocks and debris littered the way across. Dozens of plastic bags. Why would there be plastic bags all the way out here, in this rough wilderness, nowhere near civilization? How did they get here? On the way over, I'd run across the riverbed without thinking, giving chase. But now, I hesitated. I looked at the trash and the rubble. I thought.

Every pile of rocks could hide another bomb, every mound of dirt could conceal a land mine. Every plastic bag could be a trip wire. Every step could be my last.

I exhaled. No time to hesitate. Better not to think about it.

"Come on, pal," I grunted. "Oo-rah!"

I was talking to myself, really, stoking myself up. I didn't even know if Loki could hear me, if he was even alive. I pushed that idea out of my head too. My thoughts were a maze, with traps around every turn. Dragons in the shadows. Better not to think about anything at all.

I put one foot in front of the other, stumbling, but moving forward.

The idea of stepping on a bomb pushed the pain and exhaustion out of my mind, replacing one shrieking fear with a dozen others. Loki groaned at my side. Alive.

I had to get him to safety, no matter how much my chest ached and my muscles burned, no matter the risk of stepping on a bomb or how much blood I was losing from the shrapnel wound in my leg.

You never leave a marine behind.

"I won't give up if you don't," I whispered as I walked, talking just as much to calm myself as to comfort Loki. "You can do it! Stay with me!"

I was never much for begging, but just then I looked up at the sky, the hazy gray void over the mountains, and I mouthed one silent "please."

Sweat ran down my cheeks.

I told myself it was sweat.

I knew it wasn't sweat.

All I wanted was to get Loki safely on board the helicopter and get him to a doctor. I knew we'd be in trouble for running off on our own against orders, for putting the entire operation in danger. Maybe they'd even kick me out of the Corps for being so reckless.

It was almost funny.

I had never been reckless before. I guess I had Loki to thank for that. He was the reckless one.

Lesson learned, pal. Look where it got us.

I laughed. And then my knees buckled as I stumbled over the rocky ground. I fell, crashing my elbows into the earth. The elbow pads kept me from shattering my bones. I heard a low groan of pain, just beside my ear.

"Sorry," I whispered. "I'm sorry, pal."

The buzzing in my ears faded, and I could make out some other sounds now: the wind howling through the rocky crags, sweeping the snow off the peaks above me; machine guns rattling in the distance, sounding like a thousand doors slamming shut in anger.

I looked up and saw streaks of orange tracer fire slicing up a far mountain. Alpha Company must be in contact with the enemy. Echo Company was probably pulling back with their wounded. All but the two of us. I needed to reach them. The distance between us was the distance between life and death for Loki. Maybe for me too.

I had to get up off the ground, get moving, get to the landing zone. If I was still out here when the sun went down, the enemy would find me. They knew the rough hills better than I did. They could follow the blood trail easily enough and they could overtake me in the dark. Of course, by then, it wouldn't matter. If I was still out here when the sun went down, my best friend would already be dead. I'd rather stay with him then, meet the same fate.

But other marines would have to risk their lives to find us. *Semper Fidelis*, the Marine Corps motto, means always faithful. The faithful part isn't so hard. It's the *always* that gets you. Always means always. Even after it's too late. They'd come to find us, no matter the risk and no matter if we were alive to thank them.

The sun was sinking deeper, its burning crown dipping below the mountains, the shadows growing nightmarish and long.

I couldn't allow other marines to come out here in the dark to look for our bodies. I couldn't put more guys in danger.

I tried to get up, but my legs weren't listening to me. My ankles wobbled. I slumped back onto the dirt. I couldn't do it. All the doubts came rushing back at me. I couldn't stay put and I couldn't go on. I couldn't hack it.

Marines were never supposed to give up. Marines always took that last mile faster than the miles before. Marines did not accept failure.

But I was failing.

I pictured my mother on the couch in the living room. She was grieving and nodding, sad but not surprised when two officers in their dress blues came to the front door with the bad news about my death alone in some wretched valley in Afghanistan. She'd lost another man.

I hoped, somewhere in that sadness of hers, there'd be a little pride, at least, that I'd been trying to save my friend. That I didn't just walk away and abandon him. Would that comfort her at all?

And then, suddenly, a helicopter dropped from the top of a hill, fifty yards in front of me, and sank to the dirt in a cloud of dust. The dust shrouded everything in a reddish haze, and the helicopter vanished inside it.

I ducked my head to shield my eyes, and I only caught the first quick glimpse of the marines who'd come to the rescue.

Semper Fi, I thought.

They covered the distance between us in seconds. Before anyone could say anything, the dirt all around me kicked up in a tight line of bullet impacts. Two of the guys fired their own weapons back toward the ridge. The dirt stopped kicking up. Whoever had been shooting at us must have ducked for cover.

I felt Loki's weight lifted from my shoulder, felt strong hands pull me from the ground, heard them calling my name, but I didn't answer them.

"Loki!" my voice croaked out, raspy with dust and exhaustion. "Loki needs a medic. He's wounded!"

I felt them dragging me into the dust cloud, toward the helicopter. More gunfire rattled around us.

"Come on, Gus, hang on," someone told me. Was it Doc Vasquez? Why was he helping me and not Loki?

"Forget me!" I yelled. "Help Loki! Get him out of here!"

If Doc Vasquez answered, I couldn't hear over the rotor blades and the high whine of the engines. Someone packed a new bandage onto the wound in my leg, and they hauled me into the bird.

There was a lurch as the chopper lifted off the ground and peeled away from the riverbed, tilting crazily as it sped over the mountains to safety. I felt myself sliding down the metal deck toward the back. Rough hands held me in place because I couldn't steady myself. I was still groaning Loki's name, and I knew my face was streaked with tears. I felt like a child.

The tail gunner was a shadow against the landscape below, totally still as the earth raced by beneath him. He fired off a couple of shots toward the hills to cover our get-away. It felt like hours since I'd collapsed on the ground with Loki. It had probably been less than five minutes.

"Where's Loki?" I called out. "Where is he?"

That's when I heard it: a faint bark, just to my left. I reached over to scratch behind Loki's ears. The dog whimpered.

"Hang in there, good boy," I cooed at him, my voice cracking. I tilted my head back to see my friend. The black Labrador retriever had closed his big brown eyes and rested his snout flat on the deck. His ears sagged back on his head. I felt my eyes getting heavy too. I was so tired.

"Stay with me, good boy," I mumbled at Loki — my partner, my teammate, my best friend in this crazy war. I tried to hold my eyes open as long as I could, tried to keep scratching behind Loki's ears and speaking in my most comforting voice. I knew, I just knew that Loki could understand.

My lips kept moving even after I didn't have the strength to make any noise. I just repeated myself over and over, pleading for one thing, the thing I wanted more than anything in the nineteen years I'd been alive: "Stay with me, Loki," I told him. "Stay with me, Marine."